HOW TO BEAT UP ANYBODY

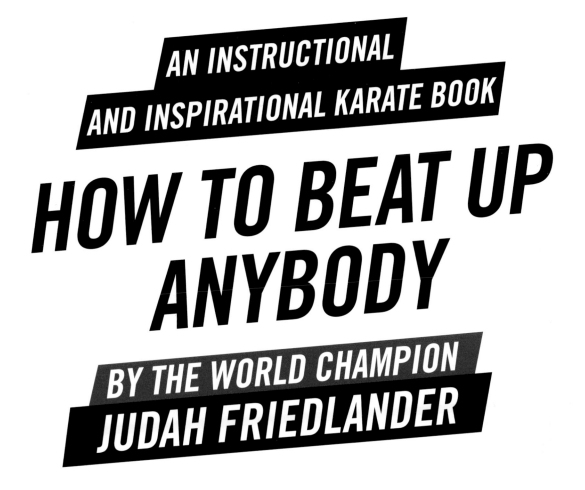

AN INSTRUCTIONAL
AND INSPIRATIONAL KARATE BOOK

HOW TO BEAT UP ANYBODY

BY THE WORLD CHAMPION
JUDAH FRIEDLANDER

itbooks

AN IMPRINT OF HARPERCOLLINS*PUBLISHERS*

THE

SMASHED TABLE OF CONTENTS

CAMPEÓN DEL MUNDO

NOTE: The above page numbers are off. That's your 1st lesson. To get good at karate, stuff can't be spelled out for you.

STOP READING this sentence and start studying this book now.

CHAPTER ZERO:
NOT THE PROLOGUE

A lot of books start off with a pompous prologue or introduction—all that boring junk that nobody cares about. I'm starting off with action. This book is about me, Judah Friedlander, The World Champion, teaching you karate.

I am the greatest martial artist in the world. This is the greatest instructional martial arts book ever made. This book can beat up any other book.

This book is dedicated to the keys on my keyboard. Because they took a beating. I broke a key every time I typed on it. My fingers are just too strong. I destroyed over 50 thousand typewriters and keyboards while writing this book.

This book is 100% written by me. Parts of it were typed using the severed fingers of my victims. So technically, maybe some coauthoring credits are due. But I don't remember their names. So forget it.

The book you are holding was not mass-produced. Each HOW TO BEAT UP ANYBODY book was made individually by me by hand. And foot. In the book, I have handwritten and footwritten my personal notes and I have already circled and highlighted the extra-important stuff. Even though this book comes pre-highlighted, you should highlight all of the words in it.

I'll admit, I'm not a strong reader. And some of you probably aren't either.

HOW TO BEAT UP

I SLEPT WITH EVERY CHICK IN THIS BUILDING. →

HE HAS NEVER FELT THIS TYPE OF PAIN BEFORE.

STANDING ON THE CRANIUM WILL DEMOBILIZE EVEN THE BIGGEST OPPONENT.

That's one of the reasons I've included a lot of photos in this book. They say "a picture is worth a thousand words." So I'd say this book has a billion words in it.

After reading this book, you will be able to beat up anybody, including anybody who has also read this book.

Let's stop messing around and get to the action.

I begin by showing you how to beat up 4 people at once. If you can learn to beat up 4 people simultaneously, beating up one person will be easy.

When you're fighting on a rooftop, you want to put on a good show. Look at all those buildings. There's some hot horny chicks in them watching from their apartment windows, and they're looking for a real man. Some girls get turned off when witnessing a violent fight. But when that fight takes place on a rooftop, 100% of them get turned on.

The strategy in a 1 vs. 4 fight is: step on the head of the biggest guy first. Then use your new height advantage to take out the rest of the pussies.

When I first saw these rooftop punks, it was this guy's fat head that I noticed first . . . and that my foot would fit perfectly on it. That's how I look at the world: "Whose head would be the most effective to stand on, work as a balancing base, and give me the height advantage, so I can beat up other people?" If you want to be a great fighter you must be able to think differently than the normal person. Without this guy's big head, this fight would've been a little tougher. Sometimes fighting 4 is easier than 3. These guys made a big mistake attacking me. I'm impossible to stop 1 on 1. But when it's 4 on 1 against me, it's more than impossible. My style is too hard to figure out. And my power is too immeasurable.

I step on his neck to take away his offensive abilities. It clips the nerves to his arms and hands, making them spasm and contort. With one move, I've eliminated the 2 main attacking parts of his body.

To get good at this, practice standing on someone's head for 1 hour straight 3 times a week. It's great training for you, but dangerous for your friend if he has a normal-sized head. So find a friend with a huge head.

I beat up the other 3 punks from right to left. I break the rib cage of the guy on the far right with one kick to his chest, forcing the contents inside his broken rib cage to spill out of it.

The guy in the middle was the easiest to beat up. He is the only one wearing a winter hat. Which means he has no tolerance for pain. If his head can't take the cold air, there's no way it can take the heat of my punch. And he's standing up too straight. Good pedestrian posture is not the same thing as good fight posture.

THIS IS PROPER FIGHTING POSTURE.

CHEST SUNKEN IN, SO YOU CAN'T GET HIT.

STOMACH OUT, TO BLOCK OTHER PUNCHES.

FEET FLAT ON THE GROUND, SO YOU CAN'T GET KNOCKED DOWN.

The guy on the left is almost as lame as the leather jacket loser. He's wearing a short-sleeved shirt over a long-sleeved shirt. If he didn't know what weather temperature to prepare for, how's he going to know what kind of a fight to prepare for? A fighter like this has no vision. If you don't have good vision, you can't visualize an incoming punch or kick ahead of time and be ready to defend against it.

Before you get into any fight, you should instantly think of at least 14 moves you can hurt your opponent with, all of your opponents' corresponding reactions, as well as 10 offensive moves your opponent might use. In this particular fight, you have to multiply all of that by 4.

From looking at the photo and reading my analysis, you now know how to beat up 4 people on a rooftop. And you know how to beat up 4 people on the ground too, because a rooftop fight is more difficult than a fight at sea level. You now also possess the knowledge of how to beat up 1, 2, and 3 persons at once. This book hasn't even officially started yet, and I've already taught you how to beat up more people than any other karate book teaches in its entirety.

By the end of this book you will be able to beat up anybody, including anybody who's ever written a karate book. Except for me. That's impossible.

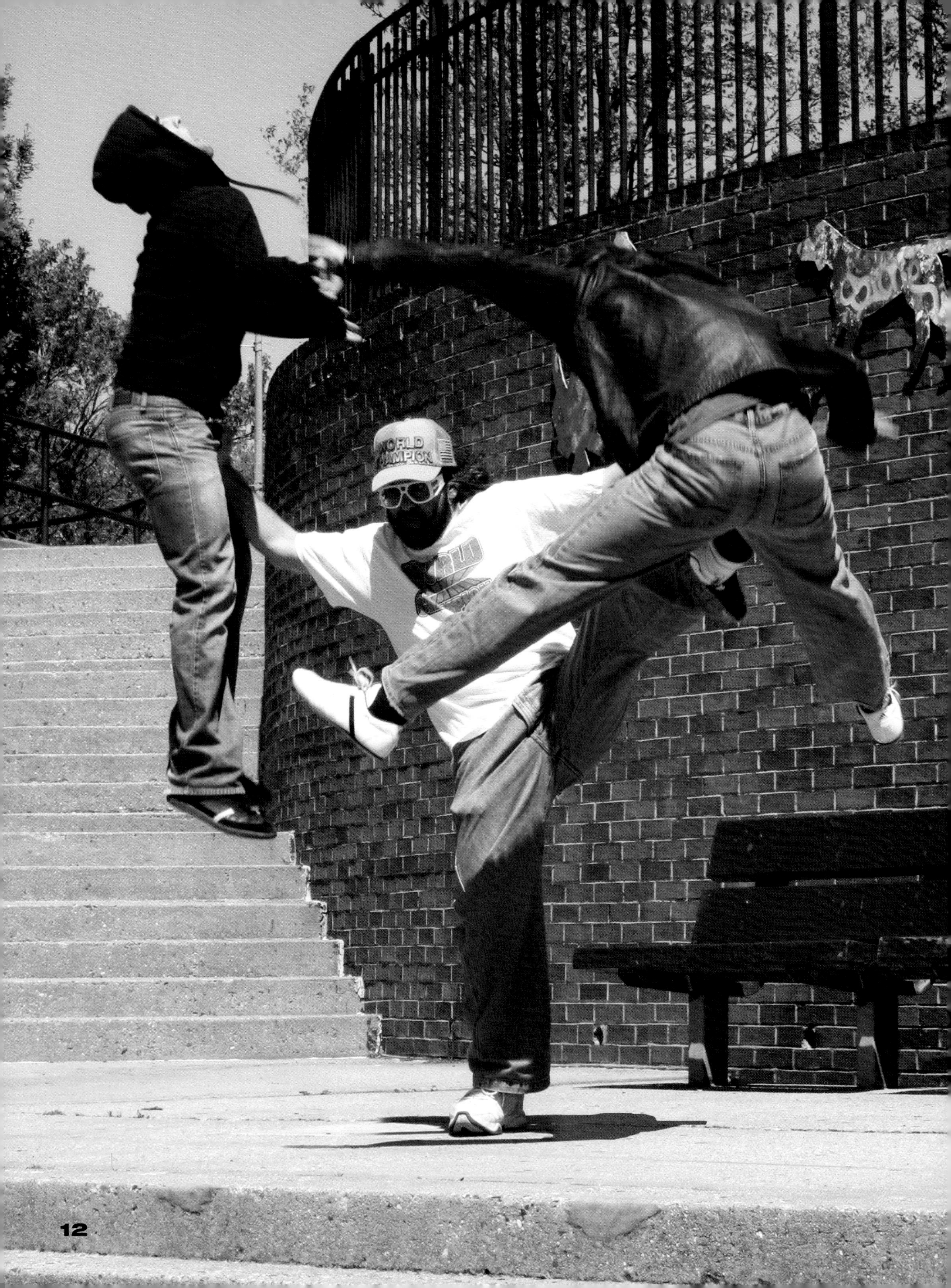
WORLD
CHAMPION

Everything in this book is real. There are no staged photos. Everything you are about to see really happened.

I am Judah Friedlander, The World Champion. I am the greatest martial artist in the world. And this is the greatest instructional martial arts book ever made. I made this book the same way I fight—alone. If you're a real fighter, you don't need help.

I am also the greatest athlete in the world, have sex with lots of women, and I'm a role model to children. But in this book, I focus on teaching you how to beat up anybody.

To make things simpler, I refer to all martial arts as "karate." And I pronounce it ku-ROT-ee. Because I'm an American.

I'VE BEATEN UP EVERY MARTIAL ARTS TEACHER IN THE WORLD. INCLUDING BERT JOHNSON.

Before the making of this book, photographing me doing karate was impossible. No one was ever able to photograph The World Champion because I physically move faster than a camera can snap a photograph. But, I have a spaceship that's also a time machine, and I went into the future and got a camera that shoots photos at a shutter speed that can capture an image at a millionth of a second. This state-of-the-art camera from the future can also time travel by itself. It went back in time and took all of the photos in this book. So now, for the first time ever, you can see my karate moves and learn from the best. In some of the photos, I still come out blurry. That's because sometimes I move faster than the camera from the future's speed of a millionth of a second. Which means I'm faster than the future. So if you see a blurry photograph of me, it's not bad photography, just great karate.

I'M TOO FAST FOR THE CAMERA FROM THE FUTURE.

I MOVE MUCH FASTER THAN 1/1,000,000th OF A SECOND.

You must realize that as The World Champion, there are many karate moves I can do that you will never be able to do. In order to make this book a relevant instructional tool for you, I have toned down my athleticism in many of the photo sequences. I have purposefully fought at a much worse skill level than I normally would, decreased my strength, and slowed my quickness—so that I can simulate the best way for you to beat someone up. I've made this book to make you a better fighter, and therefore a better person.

In other photos in this book, I will power-up and operate at full World Champion capacity. I'll be showing you karate moves that you can never execute. But don't worry, this won't make you feel inferior. It will inspire you.

There are some karate moves that I will not show you because they're top secret. And there will be other moves that I will show you, but you will not see them, because they're too fast. Do not blink when looking at this book, or you might miss one of my karate moves. Even with my state-of-the-art camera from the future, sometimes I move so fast that I am unphotographable.

I will also be teaching you methods of karate that I invented myself. Some of which were invented just for this book. So this is the first time they are ever being seen. In addition to teaching you self-defense, I will also teach you Self-Offense.

SPECIAL NOTE: Throughout this book, I use the words "him" and "his" in a way that is often gender neutral and asexual. So when I say "him" I could be referring to a male or female assailant—same thing for when I use the word "his." So ladies, just because I said the word "him" it doesn't mean I'm leaving you out. I look at all sexes equally. It doesn't matter if you're a man or a woman, you're not as good a fighter as me.

A lot of professional fighters and martial arts instructors talk about how they got started in karate. As a kid, they were fat or skinny or small, and they got beat up a lot. Then one day they started lifting weights, learned karate, and then were finally able to get a girlfriend. This is not my story. I've been kicking ass since before day one.

I was the fastest sperm that entered my mom's body. The other sperms weren't even close. I had superior speed and vision. I knew my target and I had perfect aim. These are qualities that make a karate champion.

My mom did not go into labor. After being in her womb for 8 months, I had enough. I walked out of her vagina, snapped the umbilical cord in half, punched the doctor in the face, and made him cry. I wasn't even a minute old and I had already beat up a dude. It was at this moment that I knew that one day I would become . . . The World Champion.

SOMETIMES, EVEN WHEN I'M STANDING STILL, I MOVE SO FAST, I APPEAR BLURRY.

I got kicked out of kindergarten for refusing to take a nap at naptime. I told them, "I don't take naps. I prefer to stay awake. In case shit goes down."

When I was 6, I ate the playground jungle gym, then shit ninja stars out of my asshole for 5 hours straight.

At 9, I got kicked out of the Marines for being too hardcore. I was tired of fighting alongside teammates and with weapons. I knew I could do more damage on my own.

At 12, I was in federal prison in China for a crime I didn't commit. I learned a lot of martial arts skills there. And after 6 months, I started teaching the other inmates karate. It was time to move on.

At 13, I was in state prison in the United States. I was only there because I liked its gym and workout facilities. And there were always convicts willing to fight, so it was good practice.

When I was 13¼, I didn't escape the prison. I left. I had beaten up all the inmates and armed guards with my bare hands. There was no need for me to stay there anymore. I gave the warden a wedgie in front of the whole prison before I left the premises. Then I walked through the prison gates and drove off with a bus of cheerleaders and pleasured them with some non-karate moves.

By the time I was 14½, I had already beaten up every martial arts and action movie star. But no one witnessed my destruction because I moved too fast for the movie cameras to capture it. Martial arts movie stars wouldn't last 5 minutes on the street. In a real fight, there are no camera tricks or second takes.

At 15, I was banned from boxing because I punched too hard. The other boxers would cry in the ring when I punched them. And that was a bad image for the sport, so the commission banned me. One time, as a junior middleweight, I knocked out a heavyweight with a medium-strength shoulder punch.

At 16, every professional mixed martial artist on the planet joined together to fight me at once. But they all chickened out when they saw me in the ring, naked, doing push-ups with my dick.

By 17, I was banned from practicing karate outdoors because of the definite possibility I'd start an earthquake.

At some point, I became The World Champion. I don't remember exactly when. It's been years, and I'm not good at math.

I'm the greatest martial artist ever. I am The World Champion.

If you haven't heard of me, it's because the media is scared of me, so I don't get much publicity. Other athletes never mention me, because they know I'm better than them. And no company will sponsor me because I don't do endorsements. I'm for the people, not the product.

This is a book unlike any other. I'm giving you unprecedented, unabridged great advice on how to beat up anybody.

Study this book and make your life an even greater one. If you're reading this, you're a winner. And if you continue reading, you'll become an even better winner. And you'll be able to trust your instincts, make your own decisions, and do whatever you want.

This book will change the way you live, breathe, think, and punch. If you have a closed mind, this book will open it. If you have an open mind, this book will open it even further. And it will teach you how to open your opponent's mind with your fists and feet.

This book is for all skill levels, from beginner to blackbelt. And by the way, I consider a blackbelt to be a weak, novice level. Even if you're a blackbelt, this book will take you into the unknown.

You must be ready to embrace the unknown. Because that is where cool things happen.

I DON'T LISTEN TO SIGNS. THEY'RE JUST SQUARE PIECES OF METAL WITH STUFF PAINTED ON THEM.

AS FAR AS I KNOW, THE ONLY REASON ALL THOSE SIGNS ARE POSTED IS BECAUSE THE CITY IS AFRAID ONCOMING CARS WILL GET DEMOLISHED IF THEY HIT ME AS I'M WALKING THROUGH THE TUNNEL.

CHAPTER TWO:
PROOF THAT
I AM THE WORLD CHAMPION

Some people are misinformed and question whether I really am The World Champion. In this chapter, I provide 100% concrete proof that I am The World Champion.

The World Championship is the most coveted athletic event for fighters and martial artists in the world. You cannot enter The World Championship. You must be invited. If you're one of the top fighters in the world, The World Championship Committee contacts you. If you have not been invited, you are not one of the top fighters. It is a fight with no rules. If you're alive at the end of the fight, you are the winner.

The World Championship is held whenever and wherever The World Championship Committee decides to have it. You always have to be prepared to fight. There is no time off. It's not like the Olympics, where you know where and when the event is years before it happens. You get a call, and then you have to show up within 30 minutes. If it's in Korea and you're in Kentucky, you have to get there really fast or you lose the title. That's why I own a spaceship.

The World Championship occurs about 50 times a year. Sometimes it's once a week. Other times it's 30 matches in one week, and then you're off for a couple of months.

Here are some photos and documents from previous World Championship award ceremonies which prove that I am The World Champion.

HERE'S A PHOTO OF ME GETTING THE WORLD CHAMPIONSHIP TROPHY FROM THE PRESIDENT OF SOUTH AMERICA WHEN THE WORLD CHAMPIONSHIP WAS HELD IN ZAIRE IN 1998.

I USED MY REGULAR HEIGHT OF 7 FOOT 5 INCHES FOR THIS FIGHT. YOU CAN SEE HOW MY HEAD IS HITTING THE CEILING AND I'M DWARFING THE PRESIDENT WHO IS 6 FOOT 3.

This trophy was supposed to be presented to me by the Prime Minister of Zaire but he was afraid to meet me, so he sent his brother, the South American President.

FLIPBOOK STARTS HERE! If you don't know how to operate a flipbook, figure it out. It's a great thumb workout.

Every World Championship has a different trophy presentation depending on where it's held. This tournament had the best trophy. Its figurine was modeled on what the losing opponent looked like at the end of the match. The figurine's head has been decapitated; there's a large hole in the chest; both hands are missing as well as parts of both arms; one leg is chopped off; and the right knee is totally destroyed.

First thing I did in this match was take out my challenger's right kneecap. Then I went to work on the left side of his body and ripped off his hand and leg. Then I karate-kicked a hole in his chest and donated his heart to charity. Then I snapped his right arm off. To end the fight, I picked up his severed hands by the wrists and karate chopped his head off using his own hands. I chose to chop his head off last because I wanted him to see all the damage I was doing to him. I don't remember the guy's name because nobody remembers who comes in second. Not even him. I met his parents after the match and they were really nice. They said to me, "You're the son we always wanted." I admit, my decapitated opponent's wife was a little upset after the match, so I took her back to my hotel, and she had a great time. She still sends me nude photos of herself every Valentine's Day.

The trophy has the real blood from my opponent on it, which represents passion. The cup contains all the dreams he'll never accomplish and the columns contain his forever suffering soul and his sinuses.

THIS IS ME GETTING A TROPHY FROM THE DUKE OF CHINA WHEN I WON THE WORLD CHAMPIONSHIP IN GUANGZHOU IN 2003.

MY HAT SAYS "WORLD CHAMPION" IN CHINESE. BUT IT HAS THE AMERICAN FLAG ON IT, BECAUSE I'm AMERICAN.

Even though I successfully defended my World Championship title, the Duke was really angry at me—mostly because he bet all his money on my opponent, who happened to be the husband of his daughter, Mei-Hua. Plus he found out that I hooked up with Mei-Hua before the match. I decided to make love to my opponent's wife before the match to give me the psychological advantage. The fight ended when I karate kicked my opponent's head on fire and he burned to death in the ring. This trophy is actually an urn that contains his ashes. It was a good match that lasted 3 minutes.

The other reason the Duke is appalled by me is that in Guangzhou, China, it is customary that whoever wins The World Championship gets to have sex with the trophy presenter's wife as well anyone whom he has ever fantasized of sleeping with—all while he is forced to watch from a hidden room.

This trophy isn't that big, but The World Championship is more about the honor. And the cash. I got 2 billion dollars for this one. The sign is not extravagant because the entire budget goes to the cash prize for the winner.

It was a great tournament, but that was the last time I was in China. Because I got banned.

Here's the official letter from the King of China, banning me from all of China including the Shaolin Temple:

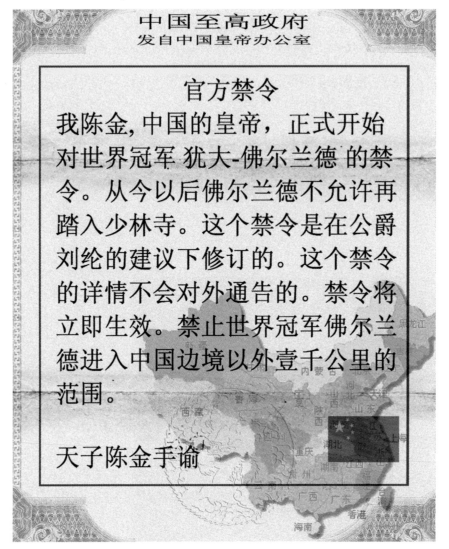

And here is the English translation:

THE IMPERIAL CHINESE GOVERNMENT
FROM THE OFFICE OF THE KING OF CHINA

OFFICIAL BAN DOCUMENT

I, Chen Jin, the King of China, am initiating this ban on The World Champion, Judah Friedlander, from the Shaolin Temple starting from now until forever. This is based on the recommendation of the Duke of China, Liu Quon. No further details will be given. The ban is effective immediately. The World Champion, Judah Friedlander, is not allowed within 100,000 kilometers of China's borders.

With royalty,
Chen Jin, King of China

I did some research, and my sources tell me I'm the only person ever to be banned from the Shaolin Temple for being too good at karate. I take that as an honor.

Like I said, every trophy presentation is different. My favorite trophy presentation happens to be one of the victories I'm most proud of. It was when I beat Cliff something (I don't remember his last name) to first gain the title in the 1980s. This World Championship was held in Carmel, California, and the trophy was presented to me by the Commissioner of The World Championship, Reynolds McIntyre. This trophy presentation was unique because there was no separate ceremony. They presented the trophy in the ring, immediately when the match finished.

Unfortunately, there was no photographer at this event. But Cliff's family was there. His 9-year-old son, Cliff Jr., made this drawing of the trophy presentation. Cliff Jr. gave me the drawing along with a big hug after the match.

Even though I completely dismembered his father and left his body parts in a lake of blood in the middle of the ring, Cliff Jr. looked up to me like I was his new Dad. He asked me if he could have some money to buy an ice cream cone. I gave him a few bucks, which freed me up, to focus on Cliff's newly widowed wife Doreen, who had been eyeballing me throughout the whole match. So we went to the locker room and took a shower together for 5 hours. Cliff Jr. was away and busy eating lots of ice cream, so there's no drawing to capture that memorable bathing experience. It's an honor when you win The World Championship and have the support of your victim's family. To top things off, The Commissioner gave me the award for Best Sportsmanship at the tournament. And declared me "the best World Champion of all time." My career was just getting started. And I've been The World Champion ever since.

CHAPTER THREE: STRETCHING

STRETCHING IS BORING. UNTIL NOW.

I'M AIRBORNE AS 3 CARS & A BIKE PULL MY LIMBS & LIFT ME

OFF THE GROUND.

It's time to start your training, but first you must learn the best way to stretch. I've invented a new way to stretch every muscle at once. And it takes less than a minute. I tie heavy-duty ropes to my arms and legs. And then have 3 cars and a bike drive away in opposite directions as fast as they can, simultaneously pulling on all of my limbs. I only use a bike for my right leg, because it's usually looser and doesn't need as much stretching. I like to have the cars go 70 mph and the cyclist go 35 mph.

While holding onto the ropes, you can also stretch your knuckles. Cracking your knuckles is popular, but bad for you. Your knuckles are your main fist-weapons. Take care of them, and stretch them out every day.

MAKE SURE YOUR FEET ARE AT LEAST 3 INCHES OFF THE GROUND.

MAKE SURE THE DRIVERS ARE FLOORING IT, AND THE BIKE RIDER IS PEDALING AS FAST AS HE CAN. YOU WANT YOUR MUSCLES LOOSE, NOT TIGHT.

SOMETIMES MY RIGHT LEG IS JUST TOO STRONG FOR A MAN ON A BIKE AND HE WIPES OUT.

EVEN THOUGH THE CYCLIST HAS FALLEN AND CRASHED TO THE GROUND, I MAINTAIN LEVITATION SO THAT ALL MY MUSCLES GET STRETCHED PROPERLY.

I have to be careful when I do this stretch. In addition to wearing out the cars' tires, I could hurt the vehicles and their drivers if I pull back too hard on the ropes.

This is the most efficient way to stretch. It only takes 53 seconds to stretch out every muscle, tendon, and bone in your body. It even stretches your veins. Stretching should always be done as fast as possible. Stretching slowly leads to fighting slowly. And you don't want that. If this stretching method hurts, stretch even further until the pain increases so much that you can't bear it. And then stretch even further. <u>Don't try this at home.</u> Try it outdoors where there's more space.

Now you know the best way to stretch. Just remember that stretching is important. But not as important as eating.

CHAPTER FOUR:
EATING

"Nutrition" is a fancy word for "eating." Eating food is important for a fighter. It gives you energy, and <u>you need energy to fight</u>. The more you eat, the more energy you will have. That's why I always eat as much as I can. And you should too.

When you're traveling, eating healthy can be difficult and it's often expensive. That's why I go to all-you-can-eat buffets. The price is great and the food is top-quality. And because the food is on display, you can inspect it before you eat it. It's important to know <u>what you put in your body</u>.

When I'm at home, I like to cook for myself. This way, I have total control over the ingredients and what I put into my body. The meal-making and eating techniques I'm about to show you will fuel you into a better fighter.

HERE'S MY OWN SPECIAL RECIPE FOR A LOW-CARB BREAKFAST BAGEL SANDWICH.

BREAKFAST IS THE MOST IMPORTANT MEAL OF THE DAY BESIDES LUNCH AND DINNER.

THIS BAGEL SEPARATION MOVE IS PERFECT TRAINING FOR DE-SCROTUMIZING A MALE OPPONENT.

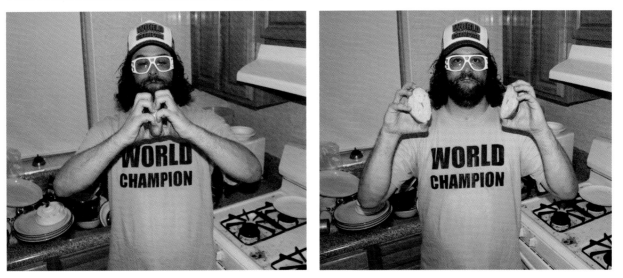

Grab the bagel firmly with 4 fingers on top and your thumb on the bottom. Then rip it in half. Using this technique, it takes about 2 seconds to rip the bagel in half. Ripping off a scrotum from an opponent's body could take up to 20 minutes. I've never descrotumized someone, because it's disgusting. But one time, I scared my opponent so much, he voluntarily de-scrotumized himself.

SCOOP OUT THE DOUGH TO MAKE IT LOW IN CARBOHYDRATES.

This scooping technique is the same technique → used to scoop out an alien's eyeball. Scoop in a circular motion around the alien's eye, then the whole thing just falls out. Because aliens have huge eyes & giant brains, there's not enough room in their head to have a strong eye socket base.

Little balls of bagel dough are also great for putting on the grounds in the woods & luring a Bigfoot into your trap.

SAVE THE SCOOPED-OUT DOUGH AND ROLL IT INTO LITTLE BALLS FOR SNACKS LATER. THEY NEVER GO STALE.

PLACE THE BOTTOM HALF OF THE BAGEL ON A PAPER PLATE AND STACK 3 BLOCKS OF CREAM CHEESE ON TOP.

Keep the top half of the bagel face down to maintain the dough's freshness while you're preparing the sandwich

I USE WHOLE BLOCKS OF CHEESE BECAUSE IT'S EASIER AND LESS MESSY THAN HAVING TO SPREAD THE CHEESE ON WITH A KNIFE.

USE PAPER PLATES. They're less likely to break than regular plates and they're easier to wash. Then hang them outside to dry. Don't bother using a dishwasher when you have your friend the sun to do the job.

Save the cream cheese wrappers. You can fold them into little airplanes and program them to go on secret surveillance missions.

PUT A WHOLE WHITEFISH ON TOP OF THE CREAM CHEESE.

FISH HAVE SOME OF THE STRONGEST MUSCLES IN THE WORLD. THINK ABOUT IT: A 2-POUND FISH IS A LOT STRONGER THAN A 2-POUND LION.

DO NOT DEBONE THE FISH. EAT THE WHOLE FISH, ESPECIALLY THE HEAD, BECAUSE IT CONTAINS FISH BRAINS.

By eating fish brains, you absorb some of their smarts and can become smart underwater. Fish have the rare ability to think coherently underwater. Top scientists in the world are smart on land, but underwater, they're flailing morons.

ADD AMERICAN CHEESE.

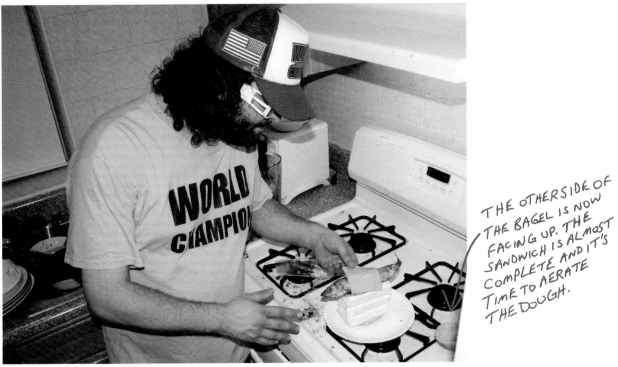

THE OTHER SIDE OF THE BAGEL IS NOW FACING UP. THE SANDWICH IS ALMOST COMPLETE AND IT'S TIME TO AERATE THE DOUGH.

LAY THE SLICES DOWN VERY CAREFULLY, MAKING SURE THE CORRECT SIDE IS FACING UP.

American cheese is the best in the world. That's why some other countries don't like America. It's not because of America's arrogance, power, or politics. They're just jealous of our cheese. America needs to share its cheese, and then there will be world peace.

Place the lox with your left hand, and use your right hand for balance. The lox seals the American cheese to the whitefish. I wear sweatpants when I cook. It keeps me loose.

MAKE SURE THE TAIL OF THE WHITEFISH IS POINTING UP. THAT MEANS IT'S FRESH.

IF IT'S POINTING DOWN, DON'T EAT IT. THIS LOW-CARB BREAKFAST SANDWICH IS NOW COMPLETE.

You can now enjoy this <u>delicious</u> breakfast sandwich that will make you a smarter and <u>more powerful underwater fighter,</u> all while keeping your carb intake minimal. And it will reboot the hydraulics of your blood system. I know a lot about eating. That's why over 40 malls in America have food courts named after me. As well as 2 in Canada and 3 in Rhode Island.

The next recipe I'm going to show you is my best. For 2 reasons: it's delicious, and it'll help make you the best fighter you can be. It is called the <u>Homemade World Champion Pizza Sandwich. Everyone likes pizza.</u> And it turns out, new studies say it's healthier than previously thought. Like cheese, pizza is one the healthiest food groups.

HOW TO MAKE YOUR OWN HOMEMADE WORLD CHAMPION PIZZA SANDWICH!

With simple easy-to-follow directions.

Step 1: Call up a pizza place and have them deliver a pizza.

I MEET THE PIZZA DELIVERY GUY ON MY ROOFTOP DRIVEWAY.

MY INVISIBLE SPACESHIP IS PARKED RIGHT HERE.

I HAVE A SPACIOUS DRIVEWAY SO THAT I HAVE ENOUGH ROOM TO PARK MY INVISIBLE SPACESHIP. AS WELL AS SOME OF MY BACKUP CARS.

You never know who's coming to deliver a pizza. So you must treat him as a potential threat.

I make him hold the pizza, so that both of his arms are occupied and he cannot attack me.

For security reasons, I do not let the pizza delivery guy come to my door. I check him out, make sure he's not a dangerous scumbag. I stand 30 feet away from the delivery guy's car. He could have buddies with weapons hiding in there. He could be hiding a gun in the pizza box.

He might work at the pizza place as a decoy to break into people's homes and commit crimes. Or maybe he's a criminal who just mugged the real pizza delivery guy, and now he's plotting to rob my apartment.

Just as I'm about to pay, I decide not to. The pizza place promised to "deliver to my door," and I will hold them to it. I will pay him at my apartment door, which is a 2-mile walk from my driveway. I decide that the delivery guy is not a threat because he's wearing shorts. Guys in shorts have no fighting ability. If you're wearing jeans, and the other guy is wearing shorts—you will win. I give him directions and tell him to meet me at my apartment. We travel separately. I still don't fully trust him.

I OPEN MY DOOR AND HIDE ONE ARM. IF HE CAN'T SEE MY ARM, HE CAN'T DEFEND AGAINST IT.

I HAVE 2 FRONT DOORS. TO CONFUSE HOME INVADERS. THE DOOR TO MY LEFT IS A TRAP DOOR. IF YOU OPEN IT, YOU WILL IMMEDIATELY DROP 75 FEET INTO QUICKSAND.

Before the above photo was taken, I got to my front door 20 minutes ahead of the pizza guy because I can walk faster than a gazelle can run. I went inside my apartment and waited for him to show up. I heard the doorbell ring, but didn't open it. I made him wait. As a martial artist, it is you that must always dictate the situation.

Always look through your security peephole to see who's at your door before you open it. I don't have a peephole on my front door. I don't need it. If someone's at my front door, I can hear him from behind my door and tell exactly what size he is, if he's carrying a weapon, his age, what kind of music he listens to, if he's got company, and if he is not a he. I listened and decided it was indeed just the unarmed pizza delivery guy. So I open the door.

As a master of the martial arts, you should be able to hear things as well as you can see them. Your eyes and ears should work identically.

I'M ABOUT TO PAY HIM. I KEEP MY ATTACK OPTIONS OPEN.

I CAN STILL THROW HIM IN MY TRAP DOOR IF I NEED TO.

MY HEAD IS UPRIGHT, OBSERVING ALL POSSIBLE ANGLES.

My right hand is free. My left hand is holding the money low, but I can still use it to strike him if necessary. Meanwhile, both his hands are occupied, and he's bent over looking down at the money. He's so obsessed with getting the cash, that he has put himself out of good fighting position. He has no idea the damage I could do to him right now. Yet, I know he's deeply afraid of me.

I'VE INTIMIDATED HIM SO MUCH, HE'S GONE TEMPORARILY BLIND.

SOMETIMES WHEN PEOPLE LOOK DIRECTLY INTO MY EYES FOR MORE THAN 2 SECONDS, THEY TURN BLIND.

I quickly cured his blindness by re-looking back into his eyes and forcing them to work properly again.

I go ahead and give him the well-earned tip that he deserves: 7 cents.

The pizza was supposed to be delivered to my door in 30 minutes, but it took him 50 minutes because of the long walk I made him take. I had an extra dime in my pocket, but decided he doesn't deserve it. He was late. Other than that he did a good job. Plus, if he holds onto those coins, in 70 years, they might become collectors' items and may become worth even double what they are today. It's important to be generous.

NOTICE THAT HIS RIGHT ARM IS MISSING. I REMOVED IT. NEXT TIME HE DELIVERS A PIZZA TO ME, HE'LL BE ON TIME.

I ESCORT HIM BACK TO HIS CAR SO THAT I CAN SEE HIM LEAVE MY PROPERTY. THIS ALSO ALLOWS TIME FOR ME TO GIVE HIM A LECTURE ABOUT TARDINESS.

We're now ready to make the Homemade World Champion Pizza Sandwich. Always order an extra-large pizza. It should be bigger than the box. Extra-large pizza means extra-calories which means extra-power when you punch and kick. It's time to add our first ingredient. Fresh tuna fish. Right out of the can.

I normally don't use a can opener. I just use my hands. But here, I'm using one, because that is what you will have to use. Use 15 cans of tuna packed in oil, not water. Most humans are made of 93% water. So we got plenty of that. We don't need more. Plus tuna lives in the ocean, so there's already water within the tuna.

DUMP A JAR OF MAYONNAISE IN THE TUNA TO MAKE A NICE TUNA SALAD.

MIX THE MAYONNAISE AND THE TUNA FISH USING YOUR HANDS IN A SQUEEZING MOTION. THIS IS GOOD PRACTICE FOR STRANGLING AN OPPONENT.

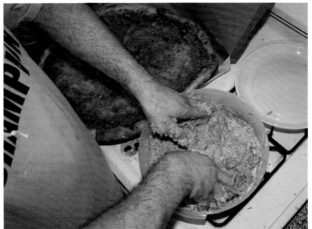

SALADS ARE ALWAYS HEALTHY NO MATTER WHAT THE INGREDIENTS.

THE OILS FROM THE TUNA AND MAYONNAISE ARE GOOD FOR YOUR SKIN. WHEN YOU'RE CHOKING SOMEONE, YOU WANT YOUR HANDS TO BE NICE AND SOFT.

Use both hands and shake the bottle really hard. This is the same technique as banging a criminal's head on the ground. Use 2 jars of mayonnaise for twice the taste and twice the banging-a-criminal's-head practice.

Do this mixing/strangling technique for 10 minutes, which is the longest it would ever take to make any mammal stop breathing.

POUR THE TUNA CAREFULLY ONTO THE PIZZA SO THAT IT MAKES A NICE PILE.

THIS IS THE SAME METHOD USED TO POUR SOMEONE'S BRAINS ON THE GROUND AFTER YOU'VE PUNCHED A HOLE IN HIS HEAD.

ADD THE MOST POWERFUL ENERGIZING MEAT IN THE WORLD: KIELBASY.

LAY THE KIELBASY PERFECTLY SO THAT IT SQUISHES INTO THE TUNA FISH SALAD.
The tuna fish salad holds the kielbasy in place. Everything in this recipe has its purpose. There is nothing extraneous. <u>Just like in fighting—don't use any unnecessary moves.</u>

I prepare this whole dish on my stovetop. You don't need a fancy kitchen to cook a great meal. The same philosophy goes for fighting. <u>Never practice fighting at a gym or karate dojo.</u> They're not real life situations, and won't prepare you for street fighting. Notice that I'm not wearing an apron or gloves. Cooking is meant to be done with your hands and clothes. You can't be afraid to get dirty. Same goes for when you're fighting.

ADD BAKED PIGEON.

GET A FRESH PIGEON OFF THE STREET. STREET FOOD WILL MAKE YOU A BETTER STREET FIGHTER.

Wild pigeon is healthier to eat than farm-raised pigeon. They're naturally cage-free. And they're also just free. Eating pigeon is the secret to staying ripped.

KIELBASY, TUNA, AND PIGEON. LAND, SEA, AND AIR.

EATING LAND PROTEIN, SEA PROTEIN, AND AIR PROTEIN WILL MAKE YOU A STRONGER FIGHTER ON LAND, UNDERWATER, AND IN THE SKY.

This is the perfect protein combination for the Homemade World Champion Pizza Sandwich.

ADD AMERICAN CHEESE TO MAKE THIS SANDWICH BETTER THAN PERFECT.

USE AT LEAST 10 SLICES OF AMERICAN CHEESE. REMEMBER, CHEESE IS ONE OF THE MOST IMPORTANT FOOD GROUPS.

ADD A TOUCH OF PECORINO ROMANO CHEESE IMPORTED FROM ITALY.

YOU DON'T WANT TO OVERWHELM THE SUBTLE FLAVORS OF THE AMERICAN CHEESE.

THEN ADD ONE DROP OF LEMON TO BRING OUT THE FLAVORS OF ALL THE INGREDIENTS.

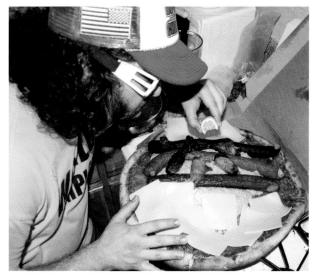

PICK UP YOUR PIZZA AND FOLD IT INTO A SANDWICH.

THE SANDWICH IS THE BEST FORM OF FOOD BECAUSE IT'S COMPLETELY PORTABLE.

Reheat the pizza sandwich. The microwave is the best man-made cooking device. This is a nice one because it has a self-cleaning feature. I also own a 25-foot microwave. Sometimes I'll get inside the giant microwave with my pizza sandwich and eat it while it's cooking.

IF IT'S TOO BIG, MAKE IT FIT.

I COOK IT ON HIGH FOR 5 MINUTES. BUT I TAKE IT OUT AFTER 3 MINUTES BECAUSE I'M A RULEBREAKER.

IT'S IMPORTANT TO KNOW HOW TO MAKE SOMETHING BIG FIT INTO SOMETHING SMALL.

WAITING IS NOT A VIRTUE. PEOPLE WHO WAIT, GET PUNCHED IN THE FACE.

THE PIZZA SANDWICH SHOULD WEIGH 30 POUNDS.

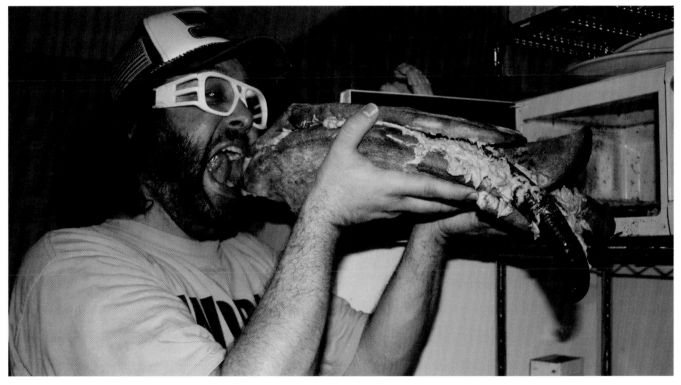

AND THAT MEANS THAT YOU WILL GAIN 30 POUNDS OF PUNCHING POWER FROM EATING IT.

Don't let this delicious pizza sandwich cool down. You want it to be as hot as possible when you eat it. It's good training for eating fire or beating up a dragon's dad.

ATTACK THE FOOD.

THE ROOF OF MY MOUTH CAN BURN A PIZZA.

Eat it as fast as you can. Speed-eating is a good workout for your jaw muscles and it makes your teeth stronger.

Do not chew your food too much. "Proper chewing" is a myth created by dentists who know nothing about karate. "Proper chewing" or as I call it, "over-chewing" is bad for your digestive system. If you only bite your food once before swallowing it, your stomach muscles will then be forced to work extra hard to digest it. And that's how stomach muscles get stronger. That's why I have ab muscles in my chest. I've gained too many stomach muscles, ran out of room, so they were forced to relocate up to my chest.

IF YOU START TO GET FULL, PUSH IT.

Always eat standing up. You cannot see an incoming enemy if you're sitting down. The best way to relax, is to never relax.

Always save some food for later. Wrap the leftovers in steel foil. Food can stay fresh for up to 6 months without refrigeration when it is wrapped in steel foil.

THIS PHOTO HAS BEEN CROPPED FOR YOUR SAFETY.

AFTER EATING THIS MEAL, I GET SUCH A RUSH OF POWER: MY EYES BECOME SO STRONG THEY CAN BLIND YOU.

And they wouldn't cause temporary blindness like they did to the pizza delivery guy. It would be permanent, and then you couldn't finish reading the rest of this book. The first 30 minutes after I eat a meal is when I am most powerful.

Now you know the proper way to cook and eat the Homemade World Champion Pizza Sandwich.

If you eat the way I do, you will be a winner. This eating knowledge I have given you is invaluable. Eat 5 of these pizza sandwiches every day, and you'll be prepared to train to become the best fighter that you can be.

It's important to always be training.

Health clubs and gyms are the worst places to train besides karate schools. Real fighters don't get in shape and get tough at the gym. They do it at home, on the streets, and out in nature. In this chapter, I'll show you the best training techniques and they won't cost you a thing. These are all methods I came up with myself and, for the first time, I am sharing them with the public.

INDOOR TRAINING: AT HOME

You don't need fancy equipment to train. All you need is your body and your mind. Here I show you how to train for strength, endurance, speed, and agility, all while working on your fighting technique at the same time. These drills don't just get you in shape; they get you in shape to fight.

Before you train, your home must be set up properly.

I HAVE A 3-LAYERED SYSTEM TO COMPLETELY BLOCK OUT SUNLIGHT: MANILA ENVELOPES, BLINDS, AND A DENIM DRAPE THAT WEIGHS 100 POUNDS.

MY CEILINGS ARE 30 FEET HIGH SO THAT I HAVE ENOUGH ROOM TO PRACTICE MY LOW JUMPS.

When you train for a fight, you don't want anyone to be able to see you. That's why I recommend that you make your own drapes—to ensure that no one can spy through your window.

The best way to train for karate is in total darkness. At first, you won't be able to see anything. But then your other senses will be forced to work harder and they will become more powerful. After a while, your eyes will train themselves to be able to see in the darkness as well. Nobody is more dangerous than a night-fighter. Anyone can learn to fight during the day, but very few can master night-fighting.

When I train at home, I generate so much heat and humidity the paint melts off my walls. The air conditioner is able to cool things down to a nice temperature of 120°.

Now that you've been instructed how to keep your at-home training facility pitch-black and 100% private, let's start with the indoor training exercises.

All the photos in this section were filmed in complete darkness.

Start your training with oven door sit-ups.

OVEN DOOR SIT-UPS

DO NOT LET YOUR FEET TOUCH THE OVEN DOOR. KEEP THEM RAISED ON YOUR OWN.

PRACTICE KARATE PUNCHES AS YOU DO SIT-UPS.

The oven should be turned on high. Doing sit-ups with 500° heat blowing in your face makes you tougher. Sometimes I'll cook a turkey in the oven and eat it while doing the sit-ups.

You should be moving so fast that after a while, you won't feel the heat from the oven because the speed of your body is generating more heat than the oven. If you do this, you will feel a cool breeze coming from the 500° oven.

This is the best abs exercise in the world. I do this for 4 hours a day 5 times a day. Try to do at least 80 sit-ups per minute if you're a beginner.

After working on your stomach muscles, you should work on your back muscles. Refrigerator back squats are the best way to strengthen your back muscles.

REFRIGERATOR BACK SQUATS

INCORRECT FORM

Here I purposefully display incorrect technique. I want you to write in the space below at least 5 things I'm doing wrong here.

1.
2.
3.
4.
5.

The back squat technique is fine, but I should be practicing karate kicks as I lift the 2,000-pound fridge with my back. In addition to having food in the fridge, I load it up with 1,500 pounds of weights. And I should be on my toes. The toes are the most underrated part of the body and one of the strongest. They hold up your body all day and spring it into action.

After doing squats, start your knuckle training with refrigerator punches.

KNUCKLE STRENGTHENING

Punching a refrigerator prepares you for a fight much more than hitting a punching bag at the gym. A punching bag is soft, and only 18 inches wide. Trust me, you will never have to fight someone who's only 18 inches wide. But this fridge is 3 feet wide, and it's as hard as metal because it is metal.

Your punches should have enough power to get the fridge bouncing back and forth like a speed bag at a pace of 30 times per minute.

Work your left knuckles too. You shouldn't be right-handed or left-handed. You need to be double-handed. And make sure you train each knuckle on each hand. Every knuckle should be of equal strength. Your opponent can never find your weakness if you don't have one.

MAKE YOUR WEAKEST FINGER YOUR STRONGEST.

PRACTICE PUSHING THE FRIDGE UP AND DOWN WITH JUST YOUR LITTLE FINGER.

After all the strength training, it's time to work on hand-eye coordination by juggling 8 cans of beans. Cans are better than professional juggling balls because they're exactly the width of a person's neck if you're choking it.

Historical fact: Juggling is not just for clowns. In the 1800s, clowns used to be the most feared fighters in the world. They wore clown makeup to hide their identity because they were wanted criminals.

WHILE I'M JUGGLING, I OPEN THE CANS WITH MY BARE HANDS AND EAT THE BEANS. THEN I EAT THE METAL CANS AND WORK ON MY TEETH STRENGTH. AND THAT'S WHEN I KNOW I'M FINISHED WITH THIS JUGGLING EXERCISE.

After your indoor training sessions, there are several things you must do. You must weigh yourself after every session.

225 POUNDS IS THE PERFECT FIGHTING WEIGHT, NO MATTER HOW TALL YOU ARE.

ALWAYS WEIGH 225 POUNDS.

MY REGULAR HEIGHT IS 7 FOOT, 5 INCHES.

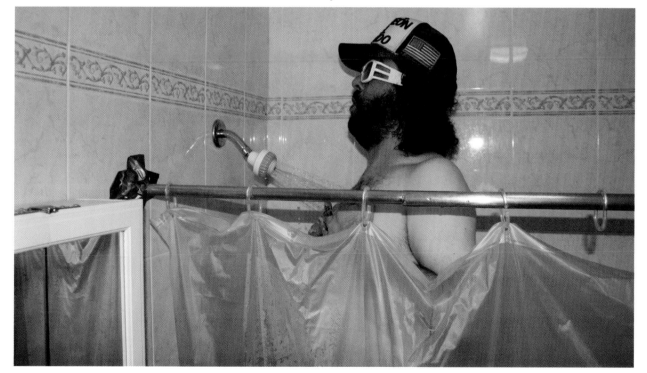

I HAVE MY SPECIAL SHOWER HEAD THAT SPRAYS WATER AT 120 MPH. THIS WAY I CAN PREPARE FOR AN OUTDOOR HURRICANE FIGHT IN MY OWN HOME.

The water temperature can get up to over 300° Celsius, which prepares me for volcano karate tournaments. You should definitely invest in one of these shower heads. It will improve your fighting.

Do not overshower. If you're training 5 hours a day, shower twice a week. Any more than that, and you're wasting water. If you shower too often, your natural skin grease comes off. Your skin grease can protect you in a fight. If you're greasy and you get kicked in the face, your opponent's foot will slide right off your face. But if you have just showered, his kick might knock you out. Studies have been done calculating the frequency of how often a person showers versus how often they get beat up. And the numbers are staggering. So, limit your showering.

WASHING YOUR HANDS IS IMPORTANT. BUT DON'T USE TOO MUCH WATER.

WATER CAN DILUTE THE POWER OF THE SOAP.

It's necessary to have clean hands so that you can get a good grip when you're choking someone. Plus, chicks love guys with clean hands.

OUTDOOR TRAINING—IN THE SUBURBS

Indoor training is great, but most fights occur outdoors. So training outdoors is essential. It gives you many advantages that training indoors does not.

Balance and strength are very important and must be practiced together.

WEARING LOW-TOP ROLLER-SKATES, JUMP UP AND DOWN ON A SKATEBOARD WHILE DOING CHEST-STRENGTHENING EXERCISES WITH STEEL COILS.

I TRAIN WEARING 230-POUND JEANS.

This exercise works your upper and lower body at the same time. It helps your balance, coordination, and jumping ability, and it strengthens your chest.

It's perfect training for a situation where you have to jump in the air and rip off an 8-foot-tall creature's head while roller-skating and skateboarding.

ROLLER-SKATING WHILE SKATEBOARDING ON A BUMPY SIDEWALK AT 60 MILES PER HALF HOUR IS A GOOD BALANCE EXERCISE.

TRAINING IN POOR CONDITIONS MAKES YOU A BETTER FIGHTER. ALSO DO THIS EXERCISE UPHILL.

ROLLER-SKATEBOARD DOWNHILL TO PICK UP MORE SPEED.

This is good training for your sideway balance. Don't always attack head-on. Occasionally it's better to attack from the side.

BREAK YOUR SKATEBOARD SO NO ONE CAN COPY YOUR TRAINING TECHNIQUE.

LATER, WELD IT BACK TOGETHER WITH THE HEAT FROM YOUR HANDS.

If you're not at the level of welding metal with your own bare hands, do not break your skateboard.

Many karate schools teach how to punch and kick. But they never teach the value of foot speed. Foot speed is crucial. The best way to get faster is to practice running really fast. There's no better place to test your foot speed than on the highway. It's important for me to be really fast, so that I can outrun cop cars and solve crimes before they do.

In photo 1, you can see me getting ready. In photo 2, I spot a red SUV and decide to race it. In photos 2–6, you can see me running much faster than the red SUV. I'm just getting started so I'm still at my jogging pace of 58 mph. If you move your feet faster than a car's wheels can rotate, you will beat it. That is the key to racing cars on foot. That's why you've never seen a spaceship with wheels on it. It's also why I have seen spaceship with feet. In general, aliens have better speed knowledge than humans.

Once I start picking up speed, I just get faster and faster. Quickness of stride is more important than the length of stride. In a fight, foot speed is more valuable than leg span. If I was running at full stride, I'd be beating this SUV by even more.

In photo 6, you see me way ahead of the SUV as I catch up to a big blue van that's going

ON THE HIGHWAY: FOOT SPEED

70 mph. In photos 7 & 8, I easily start to pass the van. In photo 9, I spot a stretch limousine—the fastest car legally allowed on the street. By concentrating on correct form, I get even faster and blow the limousine away. Stretch limousines are cool-looking vehicles, but they have yet to make one that matches my foot speed (see photos 10-12).

Highway running offers many advantages that a treadmill at the gym cannot. Treadmills don't go this fast. Treadmills can't race each other, so they provide no competition or incentive of victory. Running on concrete is better for your knees than a treadmill because it makes your knees stronger. Plus, the treadmill limits your speed and the highway lets me run as fast as I want, all while inhaling fresh freeway air. Recent tests show that running on a regular basis can lead to weight loss. So be careful, you always want to weigh 225 pounds. Remember to always hold your breath when you run. And when running on the highway, signal before you change lanes.

Racing cars on foot is not challenging for me, but it does warm me up for more intense training.

Training outdoors is essential because it puts you in real locations—where fights take place. It forces you to deal with constantly changing light and weather conditions. You must learn to obtain perfect body temperature so that you never get cold and don't have to rely on clothing. Always practice in tough conditions. I do this for other sports too. I practice ping pong in tornadoes. I practice swimming on land. And I practice high-diving into a pool with no water in it.

I DON'T WEAR A JACKET. I HAVE PERFECT BODY TEMPERATURE.

Night-running in a snowstorm against traffic is good training for my footwork in slippery conditions. I dodge cars as I run, which increases the speed of my reflexes and lateral movement.

While running, I hit a different snowflake with each punch to improve my knuckles' radar capabilities. My knuckles have become so smart and sensitive, they can feel the unique design of each snowflake as I punch them. If I shut my eyes and a snowflake lands on my knuckle, I can draw it perfectly with my other hand. High knuckle sensitivity will make you a better precision puncher.

After 5 laps around all 5 boroughs in New York City, I take my shirt off so that my chest can feel the difference between each snowflake.

I then ran 20 additional laps around Times Square and generated so much body heat that I melted all the snow. The overnight snowplow workers gave me a standing ovation. Some ladies witnessed this and got turned on. So I decided to stop training for the night and spend some quality time with the snow sluts.

By the way, I didn't need to wear the gloves and scarf. I only wore them because I didn't want to set a bad example for you.

THE AWESOMENESS OF NATURE, JUMPING IN FRONT OF THE GRAND CANYON.

THE GRAND CANYON IS 1 OF THE 10 BEST CANYONS TO TRAIN AT IN ARIZONA.

It is barren and its terrain is rugged. Even though it's 114 degrees in the shade, I wear a sweat suit, just to get my body accustomed to even hotter conditions. It is one of the driest places on earth. It's important to train at different humidity levels. I train at the Grand Canyon every day. My spaceship gets me to it from anywhere in the U.S. in under 6 minutes. It also lets me travel to other planets, where I can train under different gravity and oxygen levels, which are good for improving jumping ability and lung power.

I RUN DOWN THE CLIFF TO START MY 250-MILE WARM-UP SPRINT.

I LAND PERFECTLY AFTER JUMPING UP THE 1400-FOOT CLIFF.

Jumping up a cliff is a good quad exercise after running 250 miles at 140 mph. I did 3 sets of this workout. After the workout, I always like to sit and look at the Grand Canyon peripherally.

I LOOK AT THE GRAND CANYON PERIPHERALLY.

IT'S EXCELLENT VISION-TRAINING.

Amazing peripheral vision is what separates a good fighter from a great fighter. Strong peripheral vision will help you track multiple attackers. You will be able to see incoming punches that a normal person never could. To be a great fighter, you must have no blind spots. To get better at this special vision technique, do this: Go through the whole day only looking peripherally. Duct tape your entire face and head. But leave tiny openings by the outer corners of your eyes. Do this every day for 6 months and your peripheral vision will improve greatly.

After staring at the Grand Canyon peripherally for a few hours, I got hungry. I left my spot and went looking for lunch. A mile away I found a 30-foot-long dead python. So, I ate it. Then I caught 2 rattlesnakes and ate them alive for dessert. They're delicious. It's impossible to just eat one. After I swallow a rattlesnake, it stings itself to death so it won't have to suffer the pain that my stomach acids would inflict on it.

Now that I was feeling more nourished, I decided to go back to where I was sitting and continue my peripheral vision training. When I returned to my spot, it had been taken over by dangerous half-alien/half-human creatures. But I was prepared, because I saw them coming . . . peripherally.

THESE 2-LEGGED CARNIVOROUS CREATURES ATTACK IN GROUPS OF 3.

AND ARE ALWAYS ITCHY.

These creatures are not human. They are not alien. They are both. They are sexy, self-reproducing females and are native to the Grand Canyon. And have been haunting it for years.

These mysterious creatures remove their facial features so that they cannot be tracked by the Grand Canyon Police Department. And the FBI, CIA, military, and undercover KGB agents cannot help out because the Grand Canyon is out of their jurisdiction. But they pose no threat to me because I am too powerful and I saw them coming peripherally. I immediately get right in the middle of them.

I LEVITATE TO GET THE HEIGHT ADVANTAGE.

WHILE MAINTAINING LEVITATION, I DODGE THEIR PRIMITIVE YET DEADLY WEAPONS BY USING MY PERIPHERAL VISION TO TRACK THEIR ATTACK.

SOMETIMES IN THE HOT, DRY DESERT, MY KARATE KICKS START FIRES.

I'M THE ONLY ONE IN THE WORLD WHO CAN DO THIS.

I was victorious in this fight because of my training. You have just witnessed that a fight can break out at any time. More than 70% of fights occur outdoors. So study this book mostly outdoors, part indoors and part in doorways. I have given you the best training techniques in the world. Training is great. But nothing prepares you for a fight, like a real fight. Now I will show you how to fight. But first, I will show you some of the skills and qualities I have that make me . . . the best.

CHAPTER SIX:
POWER PUNCHING AND KICKING

MY PUNCH CAN CAUSE INSTANT MALE-PATTERN BALDNESS.

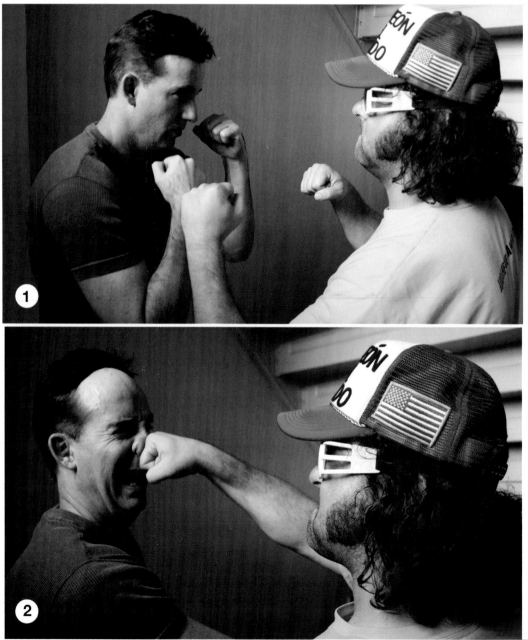

HAIRS ON THE HEAD ARE DEAD CELLS. I JUST MADE THEM DEADER.

Punching power is very important. You want your punch to end the fight. Not continue it. Punching is one of the basics of karate that many people forget about. It's not all karate chops and flying kicks.

Punching power comes from the knuckles. Your knuckles must not only be strong; they must be smart. As I make contact, my knuckles feel his nose and instantly know exactly what angle to hit him at, so that my fist makes his frontal hair follicles evaporate. Punching precision equals punching power. This is why I told you to train your knuckles by punching snowflakes. I hit this guy with a short jab. With a bigger wind-up, I could've killed him. But I just wanted to teach him a lesson. He will never recover from this. Bruises heal. But hair loss is permanent. The wind created from my moving fist pinned his ears back a little too. A punch that creates instant male-pattern baldness isn't a move I'm expecting you to be able to replicate—but it's something you should aim for.

I'm The World Champion and nobody can match my punching power.

IF I PUNCH SOMEONE IN THE CHEST, I CAN DISLOCATE HIS SHOULDER BLADE.

Here's how this particular fight went down. . .

BIG MUSCLES DON'T MEAN SOMEONE IS STRONGER THAN YOU.

BUT IT DOES MEAN THAT HE'S SLOWER.

Bullies usually take off their shirts in a fight to show off their muscles. The trick to beating up a bare-chested bully is to use his muscles against him.

I PUNCH HIM HARD IN THE CHEST AT AN UPWARDS ANGLE OF 45 DEGREES.

My punch starts an escalating domino effect of destruction. It knocks his chest muscles against his rib cage, the rib cage slams against his lungs, the lungs bang against the rear of the rib cage which crashes into his spine, the spine collides into his inner back muscles, and the inner back muscles dislocate his shoulder blade. Each ricochet of the internal organs gets more and more powerful. His upper body is a pinball machine of pain right now.

WITH HIS SHOULDER BLADE DISLOCATED, HE CAN'T MOVE HIS ARM TO BLOCK MY PUNCH.

The shoulder blade is the most underrated part of a fighter's body. Without it, a fighter has no offense or defense. The assailant's arrogant tactic of fighting bare-chested allowed me to do greater damage to him. When I punch skin to skin, my fists are beyond lethal. There's no fabric getting in the way to soften the blow. This fight lasted less than 5 seconds.

The shoulder-blade-dislocation-chest-punch is a very advanced move. It takes 30 years to master. If you're able to master it, you'll never lose a fight.

In addition to punching power, you must also have (kicking power.)

MY KARATE KICK CAN BEAT UP A BUILDING.

A CONSTRUCTION CREW IS AT WORK TRYING TO FIX THE BUILDING AFTER I KARATE KICKED IT ONCE.

WORLD CHAMPION: 1   BUILDING: 0

Your stomach hair should form a vertical line pointing in the same direction as your finger.

A MULTI-STORY BUILDING HAS NO CHANCE AGAINST THE KARATE POWER OF THE WORLD CHAMPION.

Beating up a building is not something I normally do. But the left side of this building had secretly been seized by a gang of pedophile space aliens who were plotting to take over earth one child rape at a time. For the children of earth, I did what I had to do. My one karate kick killed all the evil aliens. Earth, the planet I choose to call home, must be protected at all costs.

The construction crew trying to put the building back together was later ordered by the government to stop work. But they were not told why, because this was a top secret mission.

CHAPTER SEVEN: sIZING

"sIZING" is the ability to make yourself instantly taller or shorter. I learned sizing in 1978 when I time-travelled to 2345. I can't really explain how to do it. It's very complicated. I just have really good body control and an explosive metabolism.

SIZING is very important in a fight. A good fighter needs to keep his weight under control. A great fighter needs to keep his height under control too.

SIZING requires great concentration of your mind working in sync with your body. You have to eat a lot of calories the day before, if you want to sIZE up and make yourself taller. To SIZE yourself shorter, caloric intake does not matter.

My natural height is 7 foot 5. But if I'm just hanging out, I usually SIZE down to 5 foot 10 so that I don't intimidate people. I can SIZE myself down to 5 inches and up to 115 feet. This photo shows me sIZING up from 2½ feet to 17 feet.

I strongly recommend that you learn how to sIZE. I can sIZE up to be of equal height when I fight a dinosaur. Or I can SIZE down and go inside the anus of a dinosaur and beat him up from inside his colon. SIaING enables me to have unparalleled strength and unperpendiculared speed.

SPECIAL CHAPTER: LEVITATION

INSTEAD OF RUNNING DOWN THE ALLEY TO BEAT UP THIS DEVIANT, I LEVITATE.

Levitation is not karate. It is a tool that can give you a big advantage in a fight. Especially when launching a surprise attack from around the corner of a building. Unlike running, levitation is completely silent. The criminal can't hear me approaching.

Scientists say levitation is impossible. They're wrong. Scientists have never unlocked the mystery of gravity. I say there's nothing to unlock, you just have to overpower gravity. Now is the best time to learn levitation. With the ozone layer depleting, earth's gravitational force is getting weaker and easier to overcome.

I strongly recommend that you learn to levitate and not just because it can help you in a fight. America is getting too fat. As a result, the mass of land that Americans live on is heavier than it's ever been, and it might sink underwater soon. You better learn how to levitate so you can fly away to safety and find a place where the land has not sunk below sea level.

Levitation does not require magical powers. Just great body control. You have to push harder than gravity can pull. If you want to levitate you can't be a gravity slave. You have to rise up. Levitation takes years to master and your breathing technique must be perfect.

TO LEVITATE REALLY HIGH, I USE A FORCE STRONGER THAN GRAVITY: FEAR.

Because I'm The World Champion, the earth is intimidated by me.

I can punch earth past mars. If I threaten to punch earth, it relaxes its gravitational force and makes levitation even easier for me. But I would never harm earth. I've been living here for a while now, and I love it.

You can watch the full effect of my levitation skills in the flipbook section of this book. If you can't find the flipbook section then something is wrong with you.

The key to practicing levitation is simple. Practice jumping up—but not jumping down. You gotta just jump up and stay there. Don't be in a rush to land. Nothing elevates your karate skills like levitation. I could levitate 28 hours a day if I wanted to, but I like to be grounded.

CHAPTER EIGHT:
HOW TO BEAT UP A GANG MEMBER

Gang members are territorial and view everyone as trespassers. If you see a gang member by himself, he's probably on a lookout mission for the rest of the gang, who are nearby committing crimes. Gang members are not good fighters. That's why they have their "brothers" for backup. If you're tough, you don't need a buddy, you just need your body. A gang member's uniform is designed to both stand out and blend in with his surroundings.

THIS GANG MEMBER IS HARD TO SEE AGAINST THE GRAFFITI.

CONTRARY TO POPULAR BELIEF, GANG MEMBERS' CLOTHES ONLY SIGNIFY WHICH GANG THEY BELONG TO, NOT THEIR SEXUAL PREFERENCE OR POLITICAL PARTY.

THE GANG MEMBER BLAMES ME FOR MAKING HIM MISS THE BUS.

HE HAS THREATENED TO BEAT ME UP IF I DON'T GIVE HIM BUS MONEY. BAD SCAM. EVERYONE KNOWS GANG MEMBERS DON'T TAKE THE BUS— THEY RIDE THE SUBWAY.

THE SPREAD EAGLE NECK CHOKE

STAY AIRBORNE FOR 70 SECONDS.

There is no better move for beating up a gang member than the Spread Eagle Neck Choke, which I invented. It allows your body to focus all its energy to your center and transmit it to your hands. The best thing about it is that it can be used outdoors or indoors. Do not practice it on a partner unless he enjoys instant pain and death.

HIS EYES ROLL TO THE BACK OF HIS HEAD, LOOKING AT HIS BRAIN FOR HELP.

AS YOU CHOKE THIS PUNK, CROSS YOUR THUMBS, THEN SQUEEZE THEM TOGETHER, SMASHING HIS ADAM'S APPLE.

You've destroyed his male dignity, his ability to breathe, and he can't call for help.

HE TRIES TO ESCAPE BY OPENING THE STREET GRATE UNDER HIS FEET BUT I KICK HIM IN THE FACE.

STREET GRATES ARE OFTEN USED BY GANG MEMBERS AS SECRET PASSAGEWAYS TO THEIR UNDERGROUND HEADQUARTERS.

To be safe on the streets, you must know the streets. I could turn this gang member over to the cops or report him to the next bus driver. But I just leave him in the gutter where he belongs.

CHAPTER NINE:

Unicyclists are dangerous. They have excellent balance, are resourceful, and usually work alone—so they have to be tough. If you ever see someone on a unicycle, start Self-Offense immediately.

This unicyclist has the height advantage. He approached so quickly, I didn't have time to RE-SIZE.

A HARD KICK TO HIS ABDOMEN CAUSES HIM TO LOSE BALANCE.

BY NATURE, UNICYCLISTS ARE SHOW-OFFS. SO THEIR OFFENSE IS STRONG, BUT THEIR DEFENSE IS WEAK.

MY ONE KICK HAS KNOCKED HIM OFF HIS ONE WHEEL.

REMAIN IN ATTACK POSITION TO MAKE SURE HE'S UNCONSCIOUS.

A POGO-STICK STOMP TO THE FACE WILL DEMOBILIZE THE UNICYCLIST.

In 5 weeks, the unicyclist should wake up from a coma. And in about 2 years, he'll be 50% back to normal. By then he should be able to comprehend the lesson I have taught him: Do not threaten people arrogantly with a unicycle.

CHAPTER TEN:
NINJA ATTACK: HOME INVASION

Ninja attacks have been a problem in rural and suburban neighborhoods for years. And now, home invasions by ninjas in urban communities are on the rise at an alarming rate. Ninja attacks are up 30% just in the last 2 days. Traditionally, ninjas are nocturnal warriors who prefer to attack in groups, and wear all black so that they blend with the night. But with tough economic times, they have grown increasingly desperate, and have begun to attack during the daytime as well, often without teammates.

Ninjas claim to have invisible powers, shapeshifting ability, and the gift of flight.

They have an incredible mystique, but compared to me, a lame reality.

I will show you how to successfully defend against a ninja home

THESE CHICKS HAVE JUST FINISHED WATCHING MY INSTRUCTIONAL VIDEO "HOW TO HAVE SEX WITH THE WORLD CHAMPION PART 3 IN 3-D" AND ARE ABOUT TO SHOW ME WHAT THEY LEARNED.

A NINJA APPEARS IN THE WINDOW.

THIS NINJA IS JEALOUS OF ME BECAUSE I'M WITH 3 LADIES, AND HE'S BEEN TRAINING WITH DUDES ALL DAY.

He thinks I don't see him. But I do—in the reflection on the TV screen. I also heard him arrive at my window. Ninjas are masters at moving silently. But I was born with owl eardrums, and I used to be a security guard at the Mime Library, where I was trained to hear silence.

I SURPRISE HIM WITH A FLYING COMBINATION KICK-PUNCH.

THE NINJA'S SURPRISE ATTACK HAS FAILED.

I've never been surprised. Except twice: once when I broke my own power punching record without even trying to break it. And the other time was when I made love to 10 women in 10 minutes, but then found out it was really 12 women in 5 minutes.

MY FLYING COMBINATION KICK-PUNCH WAS A DECOY. BEFORE HE CAN REACT, I SWITCH TO A STANDING NECK-KICK.

I PRESS MY ARMS AGAINST THE WALL TO GIVE MY KICK MORE POWER.

Ninjas are well-trained in speed and agility, but not strength. That's why you've never seen a 300-pound ninja.

I DECIDE TO TAKE THE FIGHT OUTSIDE ON THE FIRE ESCAPE. I DON'T WANT THE GIRLS GETTING HURT.

I WAS BORN ON A FIRE ESCAPE, SO THIS FIGHT IS GOING TO BE EASY.

WE'RE 170 FEET ABOVE GROUND. THIS IS A HIGH-STAKES BATTLE WITH NO ROOM FOR ERROR.

NINJAS TRAIN TO FIGHT AT HIGH ALTITUDES ON MOUNTAINS AND TOWERS, BUT NOT ON FIRE ESCAPES.

Fire escapes were invented in the 1800s. The Ninja society started in the 1500s. Because of their strict adherence to tradition, they still use their original training methods and never learned how to fight properly on modern fire escapes.

I KICK THE NINJA IN THE FACE AND CAUSE DAMAGE TO HIS FACE MUSCLES. NINJAS ARE BETTER AT DEFENDING PUNCHES THAN KICKS.

The ninja now wishes he was on the elevated subway that's behind him in the distance, so he can take a ride back to ninja class. I grab the ninja's right arm with my left hand so that he doesn't fall down the fire escape steps when I kick him. Even when you're beating someone up it's important to be safe. Kick him in the face 5 times from this position. 5 is an unlucky number for ninjas. Not 13.

I PUNCH THE NINJA IN THE JAW SO THAT HE'S UNABLE TO SPEAK AND CAN'T ASK THE GIRLS OUT ON A DATE.

It's nice to have pretty girls cheering you on when you beat up a ninja on a fire escape. The girls are even more turned on than before, and I didn't think that was possible.

I tell the girls to go back inside for safety reasons. Because I'm The World Champion and there's no chance I'm going to lose, it's actually safe for them to watch. But if they're back in the room and can't see the fight, they'll worry about me and crave my body even more.

This is not a kick to his nuts. This kick doesn't rupture his testicles; it empties his nutsack of all its fluid. And the fluid travels directly to his head, drowning his brain with scrotum juice.

THIS KICK IS A "BETWEEN-THE-NUTS-CROTCH-KICK" THAT I INVENTED WHEN I DEFEATED THE PRINCE OF SWEDEN IN KENTUCKY AT THE WORLD CHAMPIONSHIP IN 1993.

It creates a severe headache, fever, frontal toothaches, stiffening of joints, and demobilization of the center of gravity in your opponent.

THIS KICK CREATES AN ECHO THAT CAN BE HEARD FOR MILES.

I could finish off the ninja right now, but I don't. I decide to prolong his agony and give him more physical and psychological punishment for invading my home and trying to hit on my women. So I give him time to recover.

THE NINJA IS UNABLE TO PUNCH ME BECAUSE I'VE ACTIVATED MY FORCE FIELD.

PUNCHING A FORCE FIELD CAN BREAK EVERY BONE IN YOUR HAND. IT'S ALMOST AS PAINFUL AS PUNCHING ME IN THE FACE.

Incidentally, my right fist is called "Facebreaker" and my face is called "Fistbreaker." Definitely learn how to activate your own force field. It's a revolutionary concept that I invented that's been around for years. Force fields are 100% invisible. On a side note, the best way to fight an invisible ninja is to become invisible yourself—because invisible people are the only ones who can see other invisible people. The power of invisibility cannot be taught. It's something you're born with. But activating your own force field can be taught. It's just very technical and hard to explain, so I won't go into details about how to do it. Just remember to practice it every day, and then you'll get the hang of it after a while.

I RELEASE THE FORCE FIELD AND PUT INDUSTRIAL-STRENGTH CLAMPERS ON HIS NINJA NIPPLES.

NINJA NIPPLES ARE DIFFERENT THAN REGULAR NIPPLES. THEY CONTAIN THE CONTROL PANEL TO THE NINJA'S CARDIOVASCULAR SYSTEM AND NERVE CENTER.

TWIST THE NINJA NIPPLES TO THE LEFT TO MAKE THE NINJA'S HEART BEAT FASTER.

THE HARDER YOU TWIST, THE FASTER HIS HEART BEATS.

TWIST THE NINJA NIPPLES THE OTHER WAY TO MAKE HIS HEART BEAT IN REVERSE.

TWIST BACK AND FORTH FOR 2 HOURS TO DESTROY HIS BODY'S BLOOD SUPPLY.

His heart has ruptured and his major blood vessels are leaking. His brain is rotting from scrotum juice. He is emotionally devastated because the orange nipple clamps have ruined the sanctity of his all-black ninja uniform. The ninja is almost unconscious, yet still able to stand because of his excellent training.

LEGEND HAS IT THAT NINJAS CAN FLY. I'M ABOUT TO SEE IF THAT LEGEND IS TRUE.

If a ninja casts a shadow that is bigger than his own body, it is considered bad luck and the most disgraceful mistake he can commit.

The ninja is attempting to transform into balsa wood so he can float safely to the ground. I think he's too injured to transform completely.

But it's a long fall. He might have time to fully shapeshift and land safely.

THE NINJA DID NOT LAND SAFELY.

THE NINJA CRASHED TO THE GROUND IN PERFECT COFFIN-READY POSITION. THE FIGHT IS OVER.

I knew these chicks would be waiting for me because I have powerful psychic nuts. Men, you can learn about this clairvoyant ability if you read my previous book "Psychic Nuts."

I proved that if you beat up a ninja properly, he will not be able to fly. My home is now safe again. Here's a couple more things to remember when fighting a ninja.

Ninjas can hold their breath for 8 minutes. Learn how to hold your breath for 30 minutes. Then you can always beat a ninja in a holding-your-breath contest and embarrass him in front of his ninja buddies.

Ninjas have about 6 centers of power. But I have a million. Try to have a lot more power centers than the ninja.

If you want to confuse a ninja, sneak into his house and steal all of his ninja uniforms. Then he'll have nothing to wear and he'll never leave his house.

While a ninja is sleeping, reset his alarm clock so that he wakes up at the wrong time and misses his mission. Do this two nights in a row and he'll get expelled from his ninja squad permanently.

Ninjas are good at 2 things: overtraining and not getting laid. And 3, getting beat up by me and my forcefield.

Ninjas are masters of hiding. Ninjaism is a hidden art. Now that you know how to beat up a ninja, you can make him stay hidden forever.

You now know how to stop a ninja home invasion.

KEEPING YOUR HOME SAFE FROM INVADERS

This stairway leads to my front door, and it is perfectly designed to thwart a home invasion.

Because there is so much junk in the stairway, if criminals were to break in the front door, they would have a hard time getting up the stairs.

This unorganized mess is actually a well-organized design. I keep one side of the stairway packed with crap and a small pathway clear on the other side. This way, if criminals break in, they would have to run up the stairs single file. At the top of the steps, I have given myself extra room to stand so that I can easily pick off the single-file attackers one by one. The extra space at the top gives me the height advantage as well as superior balance.

I decorated the walls with works of art so that the criminals have something nice to look up at as they lay motionless on the steps after I've ripped their throats out.

Follow this advice, and your home will be a much safer place.

HOW TO BEAT UP SOMEONE WITH A GUN AND A SWORD.

STEP 1: REMAIN CALM. LET THE ARMED ATTACKER COME TO YOU.

As The World Champion I don't need a weapon to defeat an armed assailant. After reading this chapter, you will be able to defeat an armed assailant every time.

There are countless ways I can defeat this armed attacker. I could strangle him with the metal tubing or use the filing cabinet behind me as a shield. But I will show you how to defeat the double-weaponed opponent with no improvised weapons.

A QUICK KICK TO THE STOMACH CAUSES HIM TO LOSE BREATH AND DROP HIS WEAPONS.

Keep your kicking leg locked and completely straight so it acts as an extension of your back. Remember, the back is the most powerful muscle in your body.

QUICKLY KICK THE WEAPONS AWAY. ALWAYS KICK THE GUN AWAY FIRST, THEN THE SWORD.

Be sure to bend 3 fingers in on both of your hands for proper technique when you kick the gun away.

BREAK HIS FINGERS.   **BREAK HIS FINGERS AGAIN.**

Fingers have lots of knuckles. Sometimes they need to be broken more than once to be fully unfunctional. If just one finger is broken, it can latch on to a good finger and still be effective. That's why all his fingers must be decimated. Now he'll never be able to use that gun.

DISLOCATING THE ELBOW IS EASY ONCE YOU'VE BROKEN THE ATTACKER'S FINGERS. DISLOCATE HIS KNEECAPS.

I look the attacker right in the eye to let him know that I am dominating the fight.

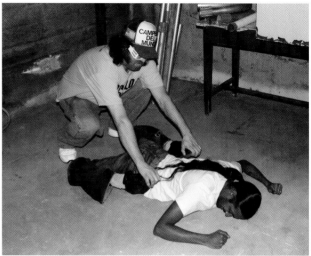

This makes a louder popping sound than the finger breaking and elbow dislocation did.

It's time to do one of the most effective moves in the world, the Tokohoojudah.

Criss-cross and pull his arms around his back so that they pop out of the shoulder sockets and form an "X" on his back.

I invented this move in 1987 when I killed a mermaid's boyfriend in a swamp fight. "Tokohoojudah" means "mermaid boyfriend killer" in Tahitian.

His left arm is now where his right should be and his right arm is normally where his left arm would be. Continue to pull hard and bring his mismatched hands together.

92

TIE HIS FINGERS INTO A KNOT.

TAKE HIS WEAPONS AND USE THEM TO END THE FIGHT.

Since you've broken all the fingers and knuckles in one of his hands, it is now possible to tie his fingers into a knot without any resistance. Double-knot it if you want to, but it's not necessary.

BUT FIRST, PRACTICE YOUR LEFT HOOK.

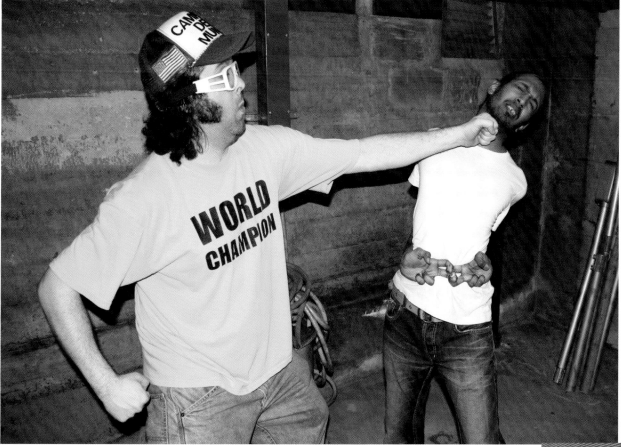

Tearing ligaments and dislocating joints are not taught in martial arts schools. But I'm teaching it to you because I care.

HOW TO DISARM A MAN WITH A GUN

Now that you've learned how to disarm a double-weaponed delinquent, disarming one weapon should be easy. A kick to the stomach will not work against a thug with one gun. Since he only uses his right hand to operate the gun, his left hand is available to block a kick. So you must use a more advanced method to disarm him.

Step 1: Charge the gunman as fast as you can.

If you don't do this fast enough, you'll get shot in the chest.

I'm moving so fast, I change the brightness in the room. I move faster than indoor light rays can travel so that I can be quicker than the trigger.

Tackle him to the ground.

Wrestle him with your arms superfast and get the gun pointing away from your body.

Tie him into a human knot, so that he cannot get out of it. Then steal his gun.

I broke 14 bones and ligaments in his body in 0.3 seconds to get him into this inescapable position.

I could return the gun to the proper authorities. But instead, I will melt the gun into a metal ball using the heat of my hands and force him to swallow it.

ADDITIONAL METHOD OF WEAPON REMOVAL

THIS ALTERNATE SUBMISSION HOLD IS MORE POPULAR IN NORWAY THAN HERE IN AMERICA, BUT IT CAN BE USED ANYWHERE.

THIS HOLD COMPLETELY CUTS OFF THE THUG'S OXYGEN SUPPLY, WHICH MAKES WEAPON REMOVAL VERY EASY.

Now you know the best tactics to disarm a criminal. Experiment with these different tactics. Have a friend attack you with a sword and a gun several times, and then you'll be able to decide which method works best for you.

CHAPTER TWELVE:
BACKYARD BIGFOOT ATTACK

Bigfoot is real. The only untrue myth about Bigfoots is that they live only in the forests of the northwestern United States. Bigfoots have secret hidden communities in over 45 states. 99% of Bigfoots are peaceful, earth-loving creatures. But every society has its deviants, and the Bigfoot community is no exception.

Bigfoots rarely come out of the woods into human territory. But if they do, consider them hostile and extremely dangerous. All Bigfoots are trained in karate. And Bigfoots' eyes have a deadly mysterious magnetic power. Never get into a staring contest with Bigfoot. If a human makes eye contact with a Bigfoot, the magnetic force emerging from the Bigfoot's eyes can penetrate the person's mind and telekinetically rip his eyeballs out of their sockets. This magnetic power is the same reason why photographs of Bigfoot are always blurry. Even from 100 yards away, a Bigfoot's eyes can destroy a camera's focal mechanism. But their magnetic powers have no effect on my camera from the future because it has a built-in Bigfoot De-Magnetizer. This is the first time anyone is ever seeing photographs of a real Bigfoot.

The event you are about to see took place last summer in the backyard of my New York City apartment.

DO YOU NOTICE ANYTHING UNUSUAL ABOUT THIS PHOTO?

THERE'S A BIGFOOT STANDING BY THE FENCE. LOOK CLOSELY.

NOW DO YOU SEE HIM? HE HAS MOVED CLOSER.

THE BIGFOOT TRIES TO STARE ME DOWN.

But his magnetic powers cannot harm me. When I was 3, I ran away from my home in the tunnels of the New York City subway system and went to the mountains and I lived amongst the Bigfoots for 6 months. My exposure to them at a young age made me immune to their magnetic powers.

He probably wants to steal my food. A Bigfoot's diet consists only of eating forest rats, rotten plants, and <u>dirt sandwiches.</u> The 1% of Bigfoots that hate humans are jealous that we have the technology to make better-tasting meals.

BIGFOOTS LOOK SLOW. BUT BESIDES ME, THEY ARE THE FASTEST SPECIES ON LAND.

DO NOT LET THE BIGFOOT GET TO YOUR BARBEQUE.

THAT'S WHY YOU WILL NEVER SEE A CHEETAH EAT A BIGFOOT.

EATING HUMAN-MADE FOOD MAKES BIGFOOTS INSTANTLY STRONGER.

BUT DO A SEMI-SPREAD EAGLE NECK CHOKE INSTEAD.

LAUNCH YOUR AIR ATTACK.

PREPARE TO AIR-TACKLE THE BIGFOOT.

DO NOT LET YOUR BODY TOUCH THE GROUND! REMAIN AIRBORNE! IT'S TOO RISKY TO BEGIN A GROUND ATTACK. IT IS MATING SEASON FOR BIGFOOTS AND THEY CAN BE EXTREMELY HORNY.

THE BIGFOOT IS TRYING TO CHANGE THE WEATHER WITH HIS TELEPATHIC POWER.

BIGFOOTS ARE VERY CLOSE WITH NATURE AND HAVE A BETTER RELATIONSHIP WITH CLOUDS AND WIND THAN HUMANS. IF I DON'T PUT ENOUGH PRESSURE ON HIS NECK, CUTTING OFF THE OXYGEN SUPPLY TO HIS BRAIN, HE COULD EMIT A MIND-MESSAGE TO THE WIND AND START A TORNADO.

The Bigfoot was unable to make a cloud connection, so it's safe to start my ground attack. Bigfoots are faster, stronger, heavier and taller than most humans. That's why I have RE-SIZED to 8 foot 5 inches for this fight. I estimate this Bigfoot to be 8 foot 1 inches tall. The average Bigfoot fight is 7 foot 5 inches. Always try to be taller than a Bigfoot when you fight one. And remember this: Fight hand to hand. Never fight foot to foot with a Bigfoot.

PUNCH BIGFOOT IN THE FACE.

DIG YOUR KNUCKLES INTO HIS BIGFOOT SKIN.

DO NOT ATTEMPT A CLAW STRIKE. BIGFOOTS BEAT UP BEARS ALL THE TIME, SO THEY KNOW HOW TO DEFEND AGAINST IT. INTERESTING FACT: BIGFOOTS HAVE THEIR OWN TIME ZONE WHICH IS NOT DETERMINED BY WHERE THEY LIVE.

THIS IS NOT AN EYE GOUGE.

I'M SQUEEZING THE SIDES OF HIS BIGFOOT BRAIN—WHICH CONTROL HIS LEGS. AND HIS LEGS CONTROL HIS FEET. AND BIGFOOT FEET ARE THE BIGFOOT'S MOST DANGEROUS WEAPONS. NEVER FIGHT A BIGFOOT WHO IS OPERATING AT FULL FOOT POWER.

THE BIGFOOT TRIES TO PUNCH ME BUT HE MISSES.

95% OF BIGFOOTS ARE LEFT-HANDED. SO I KNEW HIS FIRST PUNCH WOULD BE A LEFT HOOK. I LEAN BACK WITHOUT MOVING MY FEET. SOMETIMES THE BEST FOOTWORK IS NO FOOTWORK.

THE BIGFOOT TRIES TO YELL FOR HELP. BUT I SEVER HIS VOCAL CHORDS.

A BIGFOOT'S YELL CAN BE HEARD BY OTHER BIGFOOTS WHO ARE 300 MILES AWAY, AND THEY CAN SHOW UP IN 30 SECONDS TO HELP HIM.

I SHUT MY EYELIDS. IN A CLOSE-RANGE BIGFOOT FIGHT, IT'S BETTER TO RELY ON YOUR SENSE OF HEARING.

Position yourself so that the Bigfoot is facing east. He is weakest when facing that direction. After you elbow Bigfoot, you will hear a loud thud. That means you've knocked Bigfoot out. Bigfoots never play dead.

I DRAG THE BIGFOOT BACK TO MY DECK.

DO NOT DRAG THE BIGFOOT UP THE STEPS WITH BOTH HANDS. KEEP ONE HAND FREE FOR SAFETY.

BIGFOOTS ARE VERY HEAVY. ARCH YOUR BACK AS YOU LIFT HIM UP SO THAT YOU ISOLATE YOUR BACK MUSCLES. NEVER LIFT WITH YOUR LEGS.

I BEAT UP THE BIGFOOT IN FRONT OF THE SAME FOOD THAT TRIGGERED HIM TO TRESPASS ONTO MY PROPERTY.

I SMASH THE GRILL COVER DOWNWARD ON HIS HEAD TO GUARANTEE THAT HE CAN'T OPEN HIS MOUTH AND EAT MY FOOD WHILE I BEAT HIM UP.

I DRAG THE BIGFOOT TO MY REGULATION-SIZE BASKETBALL COURT.

BIGFOOTS TAKE GREAT PRIDE IN BASKETBALL. IT'S THEIR NATIONAL SPORT. NOT SOCCER, AS IT IS COMMONLY BELIEVED. BIGFOOTS ARE VERY RESILIENT. I CAN SENSE THAT HE'S STARTING TO RECOVER.

Bigfoots do not start a basketball game with a coin toss, because the Bigfoot community has no currency. Who gets first possession is determined by a telekinetic tug of war with the ball.

HERE, BIGFOOT AND I ARE MAKING THE BALL LEVITATE.

WHOEVER CAN TELEKINETICALLY SLAM IT INTO THE OTHER'S FACE GETS THE BALL FIRST. BIGFOOTS CONSIDER THIS TELEKINETIC LEVITATING BASKETBALL BATTLE TO BE THE ULTIMATE TEST OF MANHOOD. RIGHT NOW IT'S AN EVEN MATCH. IT CAN LAST A COUPLE OF HOURS.

BUT MY TELEKINETIC SKILLS ARE BETTER. THE BIGFOOT IS HUMILIATED.

MY ESP POWERS AND SIZING ABILITY ARE 2 OF THE MANY REASONS I'M BANNED FROM PROFESSIONAL BASKETBALL WORLDWIDE.

Special Note: In karate, it's advantageous to have telekinetic powers. Like invisibility it cannot be taught. You have to be born with it. But if you do have it, you can develop and increase your powers. If you are one of those people, I can help you. Just connect with me telepathically and I'll give you some pointers. If you don't hear back from me, it means that you do not have real telepathic powers because when you tried to connect with me telepathically, you failed.

THE BIGFOOT CANNOT DEFEND AGAINST MY HOOK SHOT.

MY HOOK SHOT IS ACTUALLY A PASS TO MYSELF.

THERE ARE NO REFEREES IN BIGFOOT BASKETBALL.

STIFF-ARM FIRST.

THEN DUNK.

I HANG ON TO THE RIM AFTER MY DUNK. THEN SWING OVER TO THE BIGFOOT FOR AN UNANNOUNCED AERIAL ASSAULT.

LANDING DIRECTLY ON BIGFOOT'S NECK SOFTENS YOUR LANDING SO WON'T HURT YOUR KNEE.

There's no recovery from this fake-hook-shot-self-alley-oop-dunk-hang-and-then-fly-off-the-rim-aerial-knee-strike. I've now won the basketball game. And I've won the fight. It's time to take Bigfoot back to the woods where he belongs.

BUT FIRST I UNLOAD ONE LAST KARATE KICK.

I KICK HIM SO HARD THE ENTIRE PLANET SHAKES.

BY THE TIME I LAND, IT'S NIGHT.

I'M CAREFUL TO LAND SOFTLY SO THAT I DON'T CREATE A 50-FOOT-DEEP CRATER.

DRAG THE BIGFOOT DEEP INTO THE WOODS. THE BIGFOOT BLENDS WITH NATURE NOW THAT HE'S BACK IN HIS NATURAL HABITAT.

FIND A SPOT WHERE YOU CAN LEAVE HIM AND OTHER BIGFOOTS WILL FIND HIM.

BEFORE YOU LEAVE, PUT A SNEAKER ON THE BIGFOOT. THIS IS THE MOST DEGRADING THING A HUMAN CAN DO TO A BIGFOOT.

BY PUTTING A HUMAN SNEAKER ON THE BIGFOOT'S FOOT, YOU HAVE SEALED HIS FATE.

WHEN THE OTHER BIGFOOTS FIND HIM, THEY WILL GIVE HIM A MORE BRUTAL BEATING AND TORTUROUS KILLING THAN ANY HUMAN COULD EVER IMAGINE.

OTHER BIGFOOTS WILL BE COMING SOON AND THE LAST THING YOU WANT IS TO START AN ALL-OUT BIGFOOT WAR.

You now know exactly what to do if you ever get attacked by a Bigfoot in your backyard. Here's some more key things to remember when fighting a Bigfoot:

Never use a gun when fighting a Bigfoot. Bigfoots have telekinetic powers that can remove a gun from your hand without touching it. The Bigfoot can then shoot you dead and make it look like a hunting accident. There are very few things more dangerous than a Bigfoot with a gun.

Even when a Bigfoot has his back to you, he can hit you in the face.

Bigfoots' shoulders are structured differently than humans'. They have full 360 degree shoulder rotation. And with their incredible sense of smell, they don't need to see you, to hit you. A Bigfoot can knock you out with a no-look-behind-the-back-punch. Because they have incredibly strong shoulders, they have weak trapezius muscles.

Bigfoots are at the top of the food chain, so they don't have much of a defense. Always SIZE up before encountering a Bigfoot because their defense against a taller creature is awkward at best.

When playing Bigfoot one on one in basketball, don't let his short legs fool you. Bigfoots can jump 50 feet in the air. You should weaken Bigfoot's legs before the game to eliminate his jumping power.

Bigfoots have amazingly rapid recovery time from injuries. A broken Bigfoot bone can heal in six hours. That's why you've never seen a Bigfoot in the hospital.

Bigfoots hate it when you beat them up with your feet.

All the techniques I've shown you here are ones that Bigfoots are never prepared for, so you should practice them a lot.

You now know exactly what to do if you ever get attacked by a Bigfoot in your backyard.

If the techniques I've shown you in this Bigfoot battle are too complex and you're looking for a simpler way to beat up a Bigfoot, take a look at this diagram I drew:

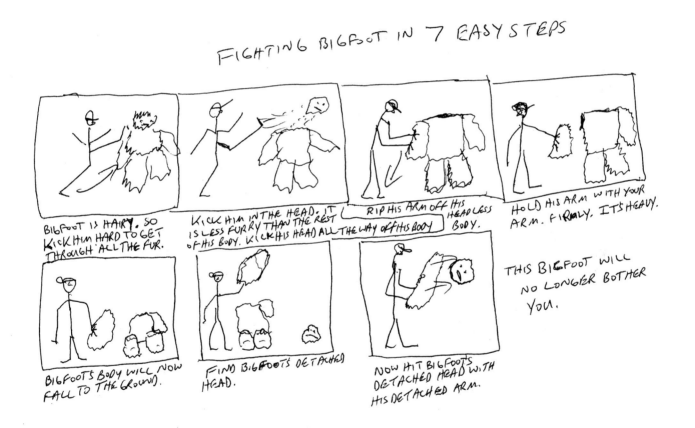

There you have it. Two different yet completely <u>reliable procedures</u> for how to beat up a Bigfoot.

CHAPTER THIRTEEN:

STEP 1. SIZE UP YOUR OPPONENT.

STEP 2. DETONATE THE KARATE FART.

The Karate Fart explodes out of my anus and instantly blinds the opponent and incinerates all the hair off his face and head. With the Karate Fart, your inner power becomes an outer force.

Notice how I get my whole body behind the fart. I lay on the ground so that I get the entire planet supporting me and giving me extra power. When me and my farts team up with the earth, we cannot be stopped. Utilizing your body's own natural power and combining it with the natural power of the earth is the secret beauty of the Karate Fart. Eating the Homemade World Champion Pizza Sandwich will give you the vitamins and minerals necessary to unleash this devastating weapon. IMPORTANT: Always aim the Karate Fart upwards directly at your opponent so that you don't destroy any plant life around you.

The great thing about the Karate Fart is that it is completely undetectable. You can be carrying it around inside you, and no one will notice . . . until it's too late. Do not attempt the Karate Fart in a real fight without practicing it on a friend first for 6 years straight. If you have not mastered the Karate Fart, and you attempt to launch one in windy conditions, it could blow back into your face and kill you.

There are many different kinds of fart attacks. There are some fart attacks that you don't want to move—you want the fart to sit in the air in one spot so that your opponent walks into it unexpectedly. But the Karate Fart is different. The Karate Fart must surpass hurricane wind power. Even if your opponent has severely clogged sinuses, the Karate Fart will unclog them, travel to his brain and kill him.

THE KARATE FART—WRONG FORM

DO NOT PERFORM THE KARATE FART STANDING UP. YOUR FART WILL BE AIMED IN THE WRONG DIRECTION AND YOU'LL MISS YOUR TARGET. PLUS YOUR FART POWER WILL BE TOO WEAK TO CAUSE ANY DAMAGE.

Done correctly, the Karate Fart is powerful. It can dull a ninja star. It can put a ninja into a fart coma. So use it carefully and don't tell anyone whom you don't trust how to do it. In the wrong hands, it could be dangerous to the whole world.

CHAPTER FOURTEEN:
HOW TO BEAT UP SOMEONE WITH ONE ARM

A NORMAL SIDEWALK.

EASY-TO-CARRY HEDGE CLIPPERS.

DISABLE THE ATTACKER.

In this chapter, I will teach you how to beat up someone with one arm. Not how to beat up someone by using only one of your arms, but how to beat up someone who only has one arm. In these 3 photos, I've powered down to fight at regular human strength. If I fought at full power, this one-armed assailant would have no arms.

These 3 photos perfectly define Self-Offense. Self-Offense is one of the most simple, effective, and practical forms of martial arts, designed to be used for common everyday situations just like this. It's been said many times that "the best offense is a good defense." I say, that in certain fight situations, the opposite is true. The best defense is a great offense. Why wait for your opponent to attack you? Attack first. "Initiate before getting initiated." That's one of the founding principles of Self-Offense.

All the photos in this section were taken 5 years ago. My clothes are different because I was working undercover to fight crime in the suburbs. To make myself completely unrecognizable, I put away my World Champion clothes and wore a white hat, a tight shirt, and really tight dark jeans instead. <u>Really tight jeans make it easier to carry and conceal weapons</u> because people never suspect that you could hide a weapon in skintight clothes. But with proper technique, it's possible.

When I see a one-armed man walking down the street, right away, I know there's a 100% chance he's looking for trouble. I know he's a warrior who's been in a fight before. He's already lost one arm. I have nothing against a person with one arm. I treat everyone equally. His one arm is very dangerous. It's as powerful as 2 arms and twice as angry. His partial arm is also a threat because it can do unusual harm with its unusual shape.

For your best learning experience, when you look at these photos, pretend you are me, and pretend the one-armed assailant is a one-armed assailant.

The hedge clipper is a cheaper and better weapon than the sword. I never buy swords. If I wanted a sword, I'd travel back in time, kill a gladiator, and take one from him. This hedge clipper technique will not work against a 2-armed opponent.

The one-armed man did not expect to be attacked by gardening equipment. And that's why he didn't know how to defend against it. This sidewalk confrontation is the most common encounter with a one-armed man. But it's also the easiest to win. There are many other much more treacherous situations than this one.

Five minutes later . . . I went to do a security check on my grandma's backyard while she was away on vacation hunting in the mountains. And I encountered another one-armed man who looked exactly like the guy I just beat up with the hedge clippers. But I thought it couldn't be the same guy. So it must be his twin. But it can't be his twin because he's wearing different clothes. And twins always wear the same clothes. I didn't have time to solve this mystery. I had to dispose of this trespasser as quickly as possible. Here's what I did:

Photo 1: As soon as I spot him, I get in fighting position. I don't want him to get the upper hand.

Photo 2: I quickly throw an old pair of my grandma's underpants that I found in the hamper over his face. My grandma doesn't have a laundry machine. She washes her 2½ pairs of underwear by hand twice every three years.

Photo 3: I grab a clay pot, which I've previously modified by lining its inside with invisible iron that weighs 50 pounds. Always have a spare modified clay pot nearby for backyard emergencies.

Photo 4: I carefully slam the pot on his head as hard as I can. If you're not careful you might not cause a concussion.

Photo 5: This is not a crotch kick. It's a kick to his full-length arm. When kicking, use your arms in a swinging motion to help you get more power. 90% of the power in your legs comes from your arms.

Photos 6 and 7: I quickly pull a golf club out of my pants. The golf club should be stored underneath the front of your pants going down the front of your leg. I did not store it in my back pocket, because I still have the hedge clipper hiding in there.

Photo 8: I use the golf club baseball style. Grip harder when you hit the target to create even more power.

Photo 9: This hit to the head has the power of 200 punches. You now know 2 ways to beat up a one-armed man. This move allows you to be the intimidator not the intimidatee. This one-armed troublemaker is now incapacitated.

I leave my grandma's backyard and a few minutes later . . . I spot another one-armed guy. He must be the twin of the first one-armed guy I beat up because he's wearing the same clothes. Or maybe he's a twin of the guy I just beat up in my grandma's backyard and the reason he's wearing the same clothes as the first guy is because he stole the first guy's clothes. And the first guy is laying helpless and naked on the sidewalk while the neighborhood is wondering why a naked dude with one arm whose crotch is bleeding is sunbathing on their sidewalk.

I'll just consider him the 3rd twin. Here's how I handled him:

I DISABLE THE ONE-ARMED ASSAILANT WITH THE LEFT REAR TIRE OF AN UNDERCOVER COP CAR THAT I STOLE.

IMPORTANT →

IT'S OKAY TO STEAL A POLICE VEHICLE AS LONG AS YOU USE IT FOR JUSTICE.

Self-Offense isn't just punches and kicks. Sometimes it involves smashing heads on the street with an automobile.

I leave the one-armed man on the street and quickly drive off and return the undercover cop car to the police department. They thank me for stopping crime. I then go to the local park to do some more undercover security work.

Photo 1: A couple minutes later, I discover another one-armed assassin practicing lethal maneuvers with some kind of a circular weapon. He could be the fourth twin. I approach carefully. The further away a twin is from his original, the more dangerous he is. He's probably not as smart, but he's definitely more psychologically unstable and stronger. I still don't know if all of these guys are twins. But I don't have time to investigate. I must enact Self-Offense immediately.

Photo 2: This is the first one-armed man I'm confronting who is armed. I must attack quietly and from an angle. He and his weapon are moving at a rapid pace. So I must attack even faster.

Photo 3: I grab the weapon and use it against him. Because it's a circle, this weapon has a limitless amount of attack angles. It's much more dangerous than a gun, which only has one dangerous angle: the front.

Photo 4: Because the weapon is so powerful, getting him to the ground was easy. I then step on his back and choke his neck with the weapon at a precise angle so that neither his good arm nor his partial arm can interfere. Choke hard so that he is unable to scream. In case this twin has more twins, I don't want them showing up.

Photo 5: I have now rendered him harmless. It is safe for me to leave.

Photo 6: But first I take his weapon, so I can study it and learn how to use it.

Photo 7: I experiment with the weapon and test it out. The swiveling motion that it naturally puts me into is a good workout for my upper abs. And to my surprise, it's a lot of fun. I think they should make a harmless version of this weapon and turn it into some kind of a toy for whole families to enjoy. It seems like a fun simple gizmo that should've been invented in the 1950s.

That was a lot of one-armed guys to beat up in 20 minutes on that one morning five years ago. I don't know if they were twins, but I do know that there is no way it was the same person. I never saw any of them again. Until . . .

FIVE YEARS LATER...I WALKED BACK TO MY CAR ONE NIGHT, AND I SAW A GUY WITH ONE ARM SITTING ON MY CAR WITH THE TRUNK OPEN.

I often leave my trunk open as a ploy to catch thieves. But this one-armed guy wasn't stealing anything. He looked exactly like the one-armed twins I beat up five years ago, but his hair was longer. So I knew he couldn't be one of their twins because he's not identical. Twins always have the exact same hairdo. He might be dangerous, but I gave him the benefit of the doubt, even though he had a suspicious look on his face.

I told him that 5 years ago, I beat up four dudes that looked exactly like him except they had shorter hair and were not as tan or as old-looking. He said, "I know." He told me his name was "Mark" but to call him "Joe." And then he told me his story. Joe told me that the 4 twins I beat up five years ago were actually not his twins and were not even related to him. Turns out, Joe had been trying to find these guys because they all copied his appearance and were committing crimes in the neighborhood—so that if they got caught, they wouldn't get blamed and Joe would. It was a classic case of identity theft. This is the exact same kind of atrocity that happens to millions of Americans every day. Joe thanked me over and over again for beating up all of his impostors. I asked him why he waited so long to approach me. He said he tried, but that every time I beat up one of his impostors, I left the scene too quickly. (Because of my foot speed training, I was just too fast for Joe to catch up to me.) And Joe didn't even recognize me until just now, because on that day five years ago, I was dressed undercover.

It felt good to have the 4-fake-twins-with-one-arm-mystery finally solved. Even though we still don't know who they are, where they came from, why they chose Joe, or how they had the technology to become duplicates of him. Joe asked if I could teach him karate. I said, "I already helped you by beating up 4 men who stole your identity, and now you want me to help you again? No problem. I'm the World Champion and I'm always here to help." He said that he owns my old instructional karate videotape from 1985, "How to Beat Up Your Dad," and has been studying it for years. So I told him that he was cool. And that we'd practice fighting as a team just for fun.

Learning to fight with a teammate is important because it helps you understand how to fight better against teammates. I call this reverse training strategy.

120

HERE WE PRACTICE A SURPRISE 2-MAN ATTACK FROM THE TRUNK OF A CAR. I OPERATE A COMPLEX AERIAL ATTACK WHILE JOE DOES A SIMPLE GROUND ATTACK.

3 FISTS. 1 TEAM.

We burst out of the trunk unexpectedly. I navigate from flying kick to flying kick without ever touching the ground, while Joe stays in the same spot practicing very basic ground tactics. I don't land in between kicks because that's a waste of time. I stay hovering 2 to 3 feet off the ground because that is the optimal height to be at when you kick someone in the face. I like to do at least 15 aerial kicks per jump. I'm operating way above normal human power here, and I'm not wearing my undercover clothes anymore. When I decide to land, I do not look at the ground. It is important to keep your head up so that you can scope out incoming attackers. Joe and I did 20 sets of this.

CHAPTER FIFTEEN:
HOW TO BEAT UP SOMEONE WITH 3 ARMS

In the previous chapter, I showed you how to beat up someone with one arm. Now I will teach you how to beat up someone with 3 arms. Being assaulted by a 3-armed person is currently a rare situation you could find yourself in. But statistics show that people with 3 arms are becoming more commonplace because of pollution, drugs, and overpopulation. In the future, many more people will have 3 arms, because they will opt for additive limb surgery. Adding a 3rd arm will give wealthy people an unfair advantage in sports. It's the steroids of the future.

But in this chapter, I will show you that two arms can be better than three. A 3-armed fighter does have one disadvantage. His brain has to choreograph three arms instead of two. This takes the brain extra time and can slow down the 3-armed fighter, especially if you get him off his game plan. One time, in the future, I had three arms added to me, making a total of five arms, just so that my brain could practice relaying messages to my limbs at a faster speed. My brain can coordinate 5 arms faster than your brain can coordinate 2. I have studied the 3-armed attacker and now I will show you how to defeat him.

I BLOCK HIS 2 RIGHT FISTS WITH ONE ARM.

There's no time to plan out your moves against a 3-armed fighter. You must improvise. Because he has 2 right arms, his right side will be more difficult to defend and penetrate. You'll probably have to start out on defense.

I DODGE 3 PUNCHES AT ONCE BECAUSE OF MY SUPERIOR FLEXIBILITY.

You have to react quickly and instinctively. If there's one thing I teach you in this book: it's to trust your instinct. Unless your instinct sucks, I say "instinct" not "instincts" for the same reason I say "instinctively" and not "instinctstively." I'm perfectly off-balance here. Sometimes the best balance is off-balance.

I LET HIM CHOKE MY NECK ON PURPOSE.

My neck is stronger than his fist and it will break his hand. I train my neck for situations just like this. To strengthen my neck, I have 10 lumberjacks surround me and hit my neck with giant logs of wood at the same time.

THE FINGERS ON HIS 3RD HAND ARE BROKEN FROM TRYING TO SQUEEZE MY NECK.

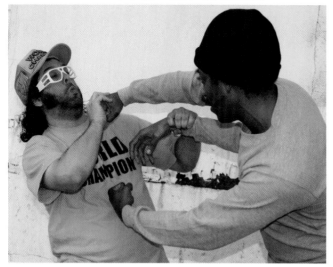

My neck is worshipped in Laos. In 1993 all paper currency in Laos had a picture of my neck on it. I move sideways to avoid his incoming left punch.

I PUNCH HIS UNPROTECTED FACE.

You have to think 4 steps ahead to stay one step ahead of a 3-armed man. When you take away an opponent's offense you take away their defense too. His left-handed punch misses. He's scared because his initial plan is not working.

HE'S BACK ON OFFENSE. NEVER COUNT OUT A 3-ARMED FIGHTER.

To block the double-fist-punch, you must elongate your fingers. In order to elongate your fingers, you must have previously stretched your knuckles which I explained earlier in the Stretching chapter. I could've dodged his punches, but I wanted to block them, to show that I have superior strength.

WITH MY KNUCKLES NOW ELONGATED, MY FISTS HAVE A WIDER PUNCHING SURFACE.

My 2 fists punch his 3 fists, which hit his face with the power of 5 fists. Even if this 3-armed man has 2 hearts, it's going to be difficult for him to find the courage to continue this fight.

HE MAY HAVE 3 ARMS, BUT I HAVE 2 HANDS MESSING UP HIS ONE HEAD.

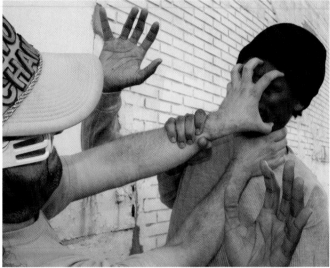

I choke the right side of his face and neck to cut off the blood circulation to his 2 right arms while he unsuccessfully tries to cut off the blood supply to my left hand. But because I stretched and elongated my knuckles, my left hand is too strong. Even if he were able to completely cut off my left hand, it would be able to stitch and re-attach itself back onto my wrist.

THE CHIN IS THE BEST PLACE TO PUNCH A 3-ARMED FIGHTER.

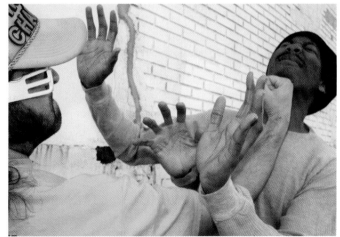

This 1 punch is actually 5 punches because each knuckle punched him separately.

HE NEEDS AT LEAST 3 MORE HANDS TO BE COMPETITIVE AGAINST ME.

I block 2 fists with my elongated left hand and unleash another chin punch.

There's no recovering from the power of my super knuckles.

It's time for me to take a walk and enjoy this beautiful city street in Warsaw, Poland. I forgot to mention that this street fight took place in Poland.

In the photos below, I intentionally let the 3-armed man get me in dangerous situations so that I could show you how not to fight. These are a couple of common mistakes people make when fighting a 3-armed man.

This is not what Self-Offense is about. It's not what I'm about. And it's not what you should be about.

LESSON RECAP: WHAT NOT TO DO

INCORRECT FORM

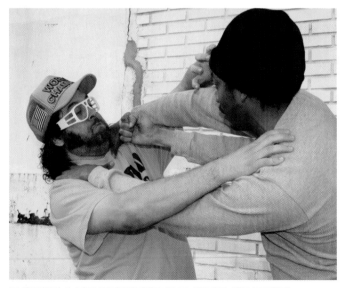

DON'T LET YOURSELF GET IN THIS POSITION.

EXTREMELY INCORRECT FORM

THIS IS THE TECHNIQUE THAT OTHER KARATE SCHOOLS TEACH. NOT ME.

TAKE BACK THE STREETS FROM MALE SCUM!

YOU NO LONGER HAVE TO TAKE ABUSE FROM STREET THUGS!

Ladies, I will teach you how to make your male victimizer the victim! From now on, criminals will be afraid to walk the streets at night, because they will know that there are women out there who have read this book.

Like the rest of the book, all the photos in this chapter are real. I went undercover as a woman in the scariest parts of New York City so that I could show you how to best protect yourself from male criminals and rapists. I RE-SIZED myself down to 5 foot, 3 inches and powered myself down to the athletic abilities of a normal adult female.

I know what it's like to be a female victim. To prepare for this book, in 1983, I went back in time to 1975, got a sex change, and lived as a woman for 2 years in Istanbul, where I was raped in and out of prison 50 times a day. <u>That was way before I became The World Champion.</u>

If you've taken a women's self-defense course or seminar before, forget everything you learned. What they teach is completely ineffective. This chapter will enable you to destroy any male scumbag who tries to take advantage of you.

Ladies, don't worry if a male perpetrator reads this chapter; he will not be able to use this information against you. These techniques are designed to be indefensible even if a male criminal has studied them.

I've dedicated this chapter to chicks everywhere.

Guys, this chapter is called FOR WOMEN ONLY! So, skip ahead to the next chapter. Only read this chapter if you want to pass its information along to a female friend or relative.

STAIRWAY ATTACK

30% of crimes against women occur in stairways. Most stairways are fireproof. Which means that they are also soundproof. And that means if you get attacked, no one can hear you scream for help.

HAVE YOU EVER COME HOME FROM A LONG DAY'S WORK, BEEN WALKING UP THE STAIRS, AND THINK YOU HEAR FOOTSTEPS BEHIND YOU?

95% OF THE TIME, THE STAIRWAY SCUMBAG WILL GRAB YOU FROM BEHIND.

DO NOT PANIC.

The stairway is soundproof. But it's not pain-proof. The heel of your shoe must be used as a weapon. Pull his arm towards you as you kick him, so you can jolt his body in 2 different directions.

BREAK HIS NOSE WITH YOUR KNEE.

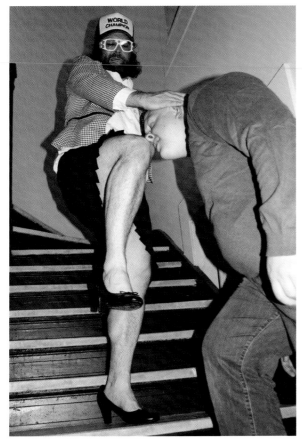

Since stairway criminals are always waiting in the dark, preparing to sneak up on a woman, they rely heavily on their sense of smell. With his sense of smell weakened, he will be easier to attack.

Special Tip:

Never blink during the entire fight. Stairway sleazebags are often large in size, but are always sneaky and deceptively quick. If you blink, you might get <u>violated</u> with a punch, grab, or tongue going into one of <u>your woman-holes.</u>

IMPAIR HIS VISION, CUT OFF HIS OXYGEN, AND RESUME DELETING HIS SMELLING POWER.

I designed this specialized move so that it only works with female-size hands. No male will be able to copy this move and use it against you.

USE COMBINATION STRIKES AT THE BEGINNING OF A FIGHT.

Later in the fight when he's weaker, you can do single kicks and punches.

USE OFFENSE AND DEFENSE AT THE SAME TIME TO KEEP HIM OFF-BALANCE.

He will overpower you if you only do defense.

THIS NECK-TWISTING-SCISSOR-SLEEPER IS AN OXYGEN-INTAKE ELIMINATOR THAT ALSO KILLS HIS SNIFFING CAPABILITIES.

WITH HIS INABILITY TO SMELL, HE HAS NO DEFENSE.

USE YOUR POWERFUL WOMAN-LEGS TO KICK HIM RIGHT IN THE HEAD. AND THEN KICK HIM DOWN THE STAIRS.

WALK AWAY AND GO ON HOME.

This lesson I just showed you works against any male attacker in any indoor location. The stairway is the most difficult place to defend yourself from an indoor attack. Once you master this, other indoor locations will be easy.

It's now time to look at how to prepare for an outdoor attack.

Attacks against women don't just happen at night; they can happen in broad daylight too.

IT'S A BEAUTIFUL FALL DAY IN THE BIG CITY. YOU JUST GOT OFF WORK. AND YOU'RE FEELING SEXY.

BUT THE CITY HAS STREET SCUM LURKING BEHIND EVERY CORNER AND CREVICE.

DO NOT BLINDLY WALK DOWN THE STREET. USE YOUR PERIPHERAL VISION.

START SWINGING YOUR PURSE AFTER THE MUGGER JUMPS. HE WON'T BE ABLE TO CHANGE DIRECTION MIDAIR.

Warning: Never carry your purse around your neck—it can easily be used to choke you. Because the purse was over my shoulder, I was able to quickly deploy it as a weapon. And be alert. Many people become victims because they are self-absorbed and don't notice their surroundings.

HIT THE ATTACKER WITH YOUR PURSE, WHICH YOU HAVE PRELOADED WITH BRICKS.

THEN HE WILL LEAVE YOU ALONE FOREVER.

YOUR ADRENALINE AND SURGING ESTROGEN LEVELS WILL GIVE YOU THE STRENGTH TO LIFT HIM WITH 1 HAND.

YOUR PURSE IS A SEXY ACCESSORY AND AN INSTRUMENT OF DESTRUCTION.

WHILE HE'S GROGGY, EMPTY THE BRICKS OUT OF YOUR BAG.

DON'T BE AFRAID TO LOOK SEXY AND FIGHT FEROCIOUSLY AT THE SAME TIME.

STICK YOUR RIGHT HAND OUT STRAIGHT FOR BALANCE.

With the purse covering his head, he won't be able to determine your location, even if you're wearing a strong perfume. In general, many men hate carrying a woman's purse, but wearing it over their head is even more de-masculating.

DO A CLASSIC KARATE CHOP COMBINATION TO THE BALLS. ONE HAND FOR EACH NUT.

THIS WILL DEPLETE HIS TESTOSTERONE LEVELS.

PRETEND YOU'RE KICKING THROUGH 5 PAIRS OF NUTSACKS STACKED ONE BEHIND THE OTHER. THIS WILL ENSURE THAT YOUR KICK GOES DEEP INTO HIS PROSTATE.

PUT YOUR LEFT HAND ON THE GROUND AND YOUR RIGHT HAND ON THE LEDGE FOR SUPERIOR BALANCE AND POWER.

YOU'VE MURDERED HIS TESTOSTERONE AND HE WON'T HAVE THE URGE TO ATTACK EVER AGAIN.

LEAVE YOUR PURSE ON HIS HEAD. IT WILL SEND A MESSAGE TO ALL THE OTHER STREETSLIME OUT THERE TO NOT BOTHER WOMEN WHO DRESS LIKE SLUTS.

Other women's self-defense books will tell you to dress down. They're wrong. It's your life, so it's your right to dress as slutty as you want. When you look sexy as you're beating up a man, he will get so confused he won't know what to do.

<u>Sexiness can be an attraction and a distraction at the same time.</u> Dressing sexy might lure in more street parasites to attack you, but now that you know how to defeat them, you'll make the streets safer for other women.

The methods I have just shown you can be used in any outdoor daytime attack.

I am the only one to ever give effective after-dark street safety tips to women. Every women's self-defense college says that for your safety, you should avoid abandoned streets at night. The real reason they say that, is not for your safety, but because they are well aware that the techniques they teach, cannot protect you. My techniques will keep you safe. Keep in mind that most purse-snatching crimes happen during the day, but most rapes occur at night. Nighttime street molestation against women is up 40%. And after midnight it's up 60%. Together we can make a change. This is the first time I am showing these photos to anyone. Including myself. They're that personal. After you have read this section, the only person that's going to be in danger walking down a dark deserted street, is the male scuzzbag that's trying to violate you.

THE CREEPIEST OF THE CREEPS COME OUT AT NIGHT. BUT THEY'RE ALSO THE MOST COWARDLY.

THEY DON'T HAVE THE BALLS TO ATTACK DURING THE DAY.

If a sidewalk slimeball tries to sneak up on you late at night, it's going to be the worst decision he ever made. One advantage most women have over men is hearing ability. That's why many women are so good at the art of gossip. Use your eavesdropping skill to hear the male molester slithering up to you from behind on the savage city streets.

NIGHTPERVERTS USUALLY ATTACK FROM BEHIND WITH A CHOKE HOLD.

DO NOT BE OVERCOME WITH FEAR. FIGHTERS FIGHT BEST WHEN THEY ARE NOT AFRAID.

DO NOT TRY TO BREAK HIS CHOKE HOLD USING YOUR HANDS.

A KICK TO THE SHIN WILL FREE YOU UP FROM THE STREET RAPIST'S GRIP.

STUDY THIS CLOSE-UP FOR PROPER TECHNIQUE.

SEPARATE YOUR BIG TOE FROM YOUR OTHER TOES FOR TWICE THE FOOT POWER.

STREETBARF LIKE THIS SCUMTOILET CAN USUALLY DELIVER A HIT, BUT THEY CAN'T TAKE A HIT.

MALE STREETGOONS NEVER WORK ON THEIR EYEBALL STRENGTH OR EYELID REFLEXES.

LEAVE HIM ON THE GROUND WITH THE REST OF THE GARBAGE AND LET THE STREETROACHES EAT HIM.

TEMPORARILY BLIND HIM AND KNOCK HIM DOWN WITH A DOUBLE-FINGER POKE.

NIGHTCREEPS ARE MORE DESPERATE THAN DAYCREEPS. SO THEY'RE MORE RESILIENT.

THIS CREEP IS CRAZY ENOUGH TO THINK THAT YOU WOULD ENJOY THIS AND THAT IT'S ALL PART OF A TWISTED FOREPLAY.

RAM YOUR KNEE INTO HIS BUTT CAVITY BEFORE HE CAN KISS YOU.

DO NOT LET HIM POLLUTE YOUR WOMANHOOD.

Point your index finger to measure current wind conditions.

GRACEFULLY ESCAPE WHILE HE WRITHES IN PAIN.

IT'S IMPORTANT TO KEEP YOUR FEMININE DIGNITY INTACT AND STAY GLAMOROUS WHILE YOU'RE BEING SEXUALLY ASSAULTED.

LAUNCH A SOARING-SANDAL STOMP.

BUT DO A BUTT-BOMB INSTEAD.

IN A FIGHT YOU HAVE TO USE YOUR BRAIN. AND SOMETIMES YOU HAVE TO USE YOUR BUTT.

CRACK HIS HEAD ON A CONCRETE WALL'S EDGE.

LUG HIM OVER TO SOME SCAFFOLDING.

STICK HIS HEAD THROUGH A TRIANGULAR OPENING AND SEVER HIS NECK TENDONS.

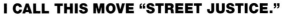

CONTINUE YOUR RETRIBUTION.

OPEN-TOED SANDALS ARE GREAT FOR CLIMBING SCAFFOLDING.

I CALL THIS MOVE "STREET JUSTICE."

THIS MOVE REQUIRES REALLY FIRM THIGHS.

THIS TOWERING STREET MUTANT IS NOT USED TO GETTING ATTACKED FROM ABOVE.

THE MORAL OF THIS PHOTO IS "NEVER STOP ATTACKING."

IT'S SAFE TO GO HOME NOW. HE IS 100% DEFENSELESS AND 200% OFFENSELESS. BUT KEEP DOING THIS ALL NIGHT.

All the photos in this chapter take place in the city. If you don't live in a city, just imagine that these photos take place in a suburb or on a farm. The location is different, but the tactics are the same.

Before closing out this chapter, I want to discuss another issue. Wearing head-phones. All newscasters and safety manuals warn women about the dangers of wearing headphones while walking alone at night. I disrespectfully disagree. If you know how to defend yourself properly as I have just shown you, wearing headphones and listening to your favorite song while beating the shit out of a mugger can be motivating and inspirational for you. Additionally, you can use the act of wearing headphones to set a trap and lure your male attacker to you. If a male mugger sees that you're wearing headphones, he'll assume that you can't hear him sneaking up on you because you're listening to music. But, if you have the volume turned down to zero, you'll be able to hear him perfectly. And you'll defeat him with a surprise counter-attack.

So there you have it ladies, the full unabridged version of The World Champion's Safety Tips For Women Only. Plus a few extra pointers. So, it's actually more comprehensive than unabridged. Even if you only weigh 100 pounds, you now know how to beat up a 200 pound man. Remember this: <u>Your violence equals your</u> attacker's silence. Carrying this book with you does not reduce the risk of an assault against you. It eliminates it 100%.

Ladies, you have all done an excellent job studying this intense chapter. If you're feeling overwhelmed from all the knowledge I have given you, that's totally normal. Since you have worked so hard, I now reward you with this full-page poster of me.

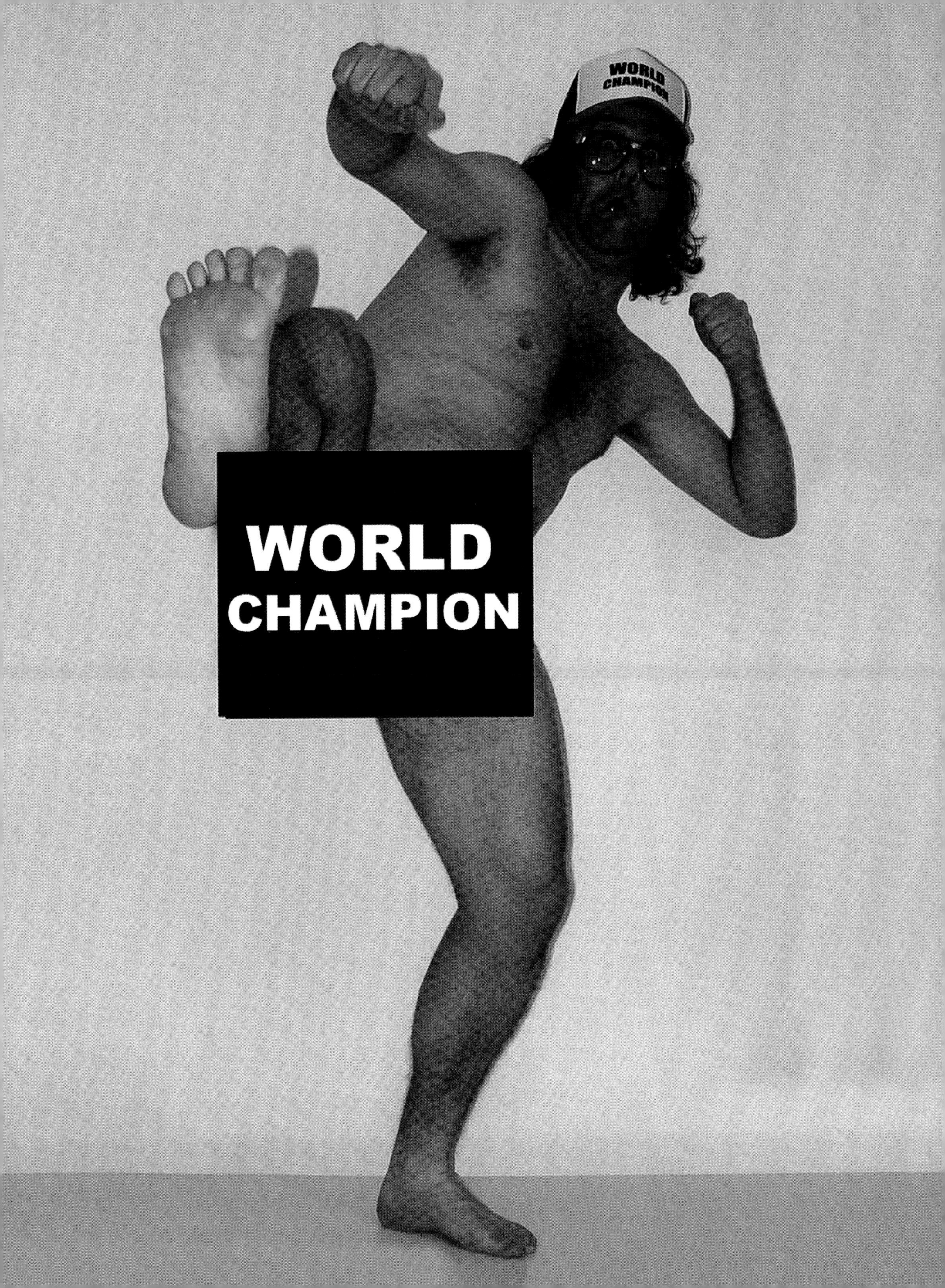
WORLD CHAMPION
WORLD
CHAMPION

I've already given you a lot of information in this book. Do not get caught up in memorizing so many different fighting styles and philosophies that you forget to use proper technique. Without proper technique, your karate kicks and punches will have no power.

These photos were taken several years ago when I was working undercover in a small mid-western town, protecting it from dinosaurs that had fallen through a time warp. When I work undercover, in order to hide my identity, I do not wear my World Champion gear. If this T-Rex saw me wearing my World Champion hat, he would have run away scared. With proper technique my power is limitless.

THIS TYRANNOSAURUS REX CANNOT BLOCK MY KARATE KICK BECAUSE I USED PROPER TECHNIQUE.

Proper technique requires total concentration.

STUDY MY PROPER TECHNIQUE FROM THIS ANGLE TOO.

After I defeated this big lizard, I took him back in time so he could be with his family. While I was there I met a cavewoman and we did it dino-style. But before that . . .

I HAD TO RESCUE SOME GIRAFFES WHO WERE TRAPPED IN A MINIATURE COLF COURSE.

It's horrible when giant animals get trapped in such a tiny place. So I freed them. As The World Champion, I must use my powers for justice. Remember: be kind to animals because humans are animals too.

151

CHAPTER EIGHTEEN: SUBWAY SURVIVAL

THE SUBWAY IS THE FASTEST WAY TO TRAVEL IN THE BIG CITY. . .

. . . AND THE MOST DANGEROUS.

You're deep below the earth's surface with no one to help you. You can't call a friend. There's no cell phone reception. There are no cops around. The subway conductor—like all subway conductors—knows karate, but he's unaware of what is going on. Plus, he's not allowed to help because it's against union rules for a subway conductor to disrupt a fight.

I LET THE GANG SURROUND ME. THEY'RE EASIER TO BEAT UP IF THEY'RE IN A SEMICIRCLE.

I recognize that they're wearing the same uniform as the gang member who I wasted on the street (see chapter 8). This gang wants revenge because I beat up their "brother."

MY FOOT IS MOVING FASTER THAN ANY FOOT HAS EVER MOVED. AND THAT INCLUDES ANY LAND, SEA, AIR, OR SPACE CREATURE THAT HAS A FOOT.

Keep an eye on the ceiling vent. There could be more gang members hiding up there waiting to attack, or it could be where they stash their weapons.

My right knee has 2 kneecaps. That's why I can do double the damage.

This gang does everything together, including executing shitty defense at the same time.

I could end this fight right now but I want to send these punks a message.

The necks of these 2 thugs help my balance as I kick the 3rd thug in the stomach.

I'm not choking these 2 thugs. I'm rearranging the vertebrae in their necks.

MY HEAD SPEED IS FASTER THAN THEIR FIST SPEED.

I KNOCK OUT 2 GUYS WITHOUT THROWING ONE PUNCH.

Making your opponent miss is a great confidence crusher. But if your timing is off, you'll get your brains knocked out.

You do not need to see the fists to dodge the fists. Use your ears to hear the fists coming towards you. Use your skin sensors to feel the air created by the moving fists. Calculate the speed of the incoming fists based on the amount of wind they generate. Use your sense of smell to determine which knuckle is on course to hit you first. Remember, every knuckle smells different. And as always, use your instinct. Even if I had no face and no skin, I would still be able to track the incoming fists. Because I have above-top-notch instinct.

IT LOOKS LIKE BACKUP HELP FOR THE GANG HAS ARRIVED. THIS MUST BE THE LEADER OF THE GANG.

The <u>gang leader</u> is the <u>most skilled fighter in the gang</u> and only shows up in emergencies. I just beat up 4 of his followers, including the female gang member who undoubtedly is his woman. To take out the leader, I must change tactics and get more aggressive.

I ATTACK HIS FACE AND NECK.

I'M CAREFUL NOT TO HIT HIM TOO HARD. I DON'T WANT TO KNOCK THE TRAIN OFF ITS TRACKS.

SPECIAL REVERSE ANGLE.

THE SLOPED RAILING IS A WONDERFUL TOOL FOR HELPING ME CRUSH HIS NECK. THIS CREATES A HEADACHE THAT LASTS FOR ABOUT 6 YEARS.

LAYING HIM ON THE BENCH MAKES IT EASY FOR ME TO BREAK HIS ARM.

SUBWAY DOORS ARE HEAVY AND WELL DESIGNED FOR EXECUTING THIS MOVE.

DON'T LEAVE HIM IN THIS POSITION TOO LONG. THE FRESH SUBWAY-AIR MIGHT REJUVENATE HIM.

THE HORIZONTAL BAR LETS ME DAMAGE A DIFFERENT PART OF HIS NECK.

I CHOKE WITH ONE ARM SO THAT MY OTHER IS AVAILABLE TO FIGHT OTHER GANG MEMBERS IF THEY RECOVER.

MY TECHNIQUE IS SO IMPRESSIVE: IN THE MIDDLE OF THE FIGHT, ONE OF THE GANG MEMBERS TAKES A PHOTO OF ME BEATING UP HIS LEADER.

The lights go out. It's pitch-black.

Because of my at-home-training-in-the-dark, I am prepared.

As the rain speeds through the tunnels, the lighting is constantly changing. In the 1.5 seconds that it's pitch-black, I have perfect vision. I notice that the gang cannot see anything yet they are starting to physically recover. Then the lights suddenly come back on.

I USE MY CAMOUFLAGE SKILLS SO THEY CANNOT FIND ME.

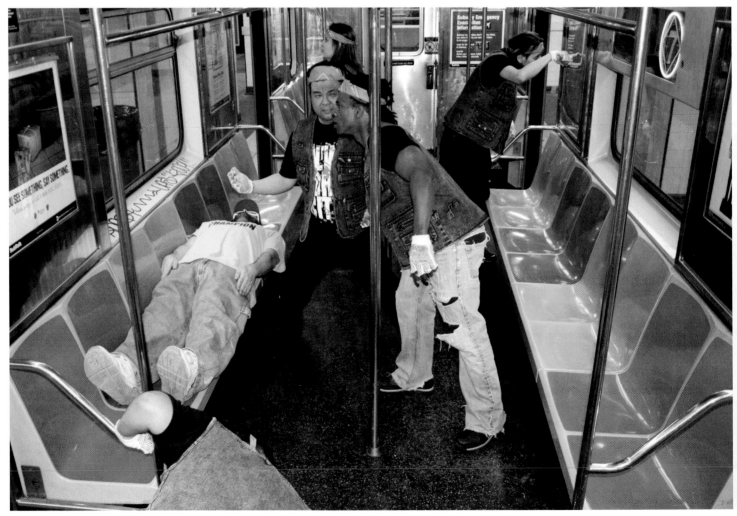

I AM PERFECTLY BLENDED IN WITH THE COLOR SCHEME OF THE SUBWAY SEATS

It's a rookie mistake to think of camouflage as a defensive technique. Used correctly, it is an offensive skill. While you are camouflaged, you are able to gain information about your attackers

Before they can locate me, the lights go out again.

I have perfect vision. Even if I remove my eyes I can see in the dark.
As a teenager, I trained myself to see with my feet.

The lights come back on. The gang is able to see me and they try to attack. But they all miss because they lose their balance when the train suddenly jolts as it takes a sharp twist down the tunnel.

I remain in my spot with perfect balance. The roller-skating-on-top-of-a-skateboard balance exercise has prepared me for this situation.

I don't have a name for this move. I improvised it right on the spot.

I pretend to look right but I'm really looking left.

I'm still working the neck of the leader.

If both your arms are occupied, that means your feet are available to fight.

The signs on the door say "do not hold door" and "do not lean on door." But they say nothing about smashing someone's face against the door with your foot. If you look closely, you can see your reflection in the metal door, which gives you a nice opportunity to check your form as you beat someone up.

This is the Princess of Korea's favorite move.

No other book dares to teach you this.

IF SOMEONE TRIES TO KICK ME, HE WILL MISS.

AND I WILL KICK HIM.

BECAUSE HE'S UPSIDE DOWN, THIS REGULAR KICK FEELS LIKE A MORE PAINFUL INVERTED KICK.

I hover in the air by flapping my feet back and forth at twice the speed of a hummingbird's wings if they were going five times as fast as they possibly could. I'm transmitting psychokinetic power from my fists to his testicles, making them rotate within their sack at high speed. Basically, I've turned his nutsack into a blender. I'm just providing the power supply. I invented this move and it is still illegal in France and Japan. Warning: Careful attempting this on a moving train. You could lose your balance and accidentally do this to your own testicles. And note that foot-hovering is not the same thing as levitation.

THIS MOVE BURNS 100,000 CALORIES.

EXECUTE THE EXECUTION EFFICIENTLY.

UNDETECTABLE

This gang will not mess with me or anyone else ever again. I can become their leader if I want. But I prefer to ride the subway alone.

I've given you all the physical and tactical ingredients needed to defeat a subway gang. Subway survival is now achievable. You never have to be afraid to use public transportation again. All of these moves translate to the bus as well. Here's a few more things you should know:

80% of subway gang attacks occur on Tuesday nights. Gang members are easier to beat up if they're on the ground. So before you fight a gang, ask them to lay on the ground first.

When choking someone on the subway, choke hard. The train ride is bumpy and you don't want to lose your grip. Subway trains are extremely loud. Don't let this disrupt your concentration. I trained for fighting in loud conditions by living inside an active garbage truck for 6 years. Always get in the last car of the train. It's the most dangerous. So you'll have more opportunities to practice karate.

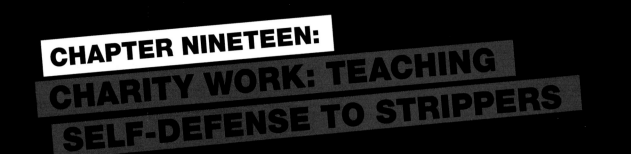

CHAPTER NINETEEN:
CHARITY WORK: TEACHING SELF-DEFENSE TO STRIPPERS

It's important to do charity work and give back to society. That's why I teach self-defense to strippers. I teach twice a day because I care about strippers twice as much as the regular person does.

Being an exotic dancer means you are a woman who is lusted after, constantly desired by men, and always in potential danger. As The World Champion, I have an incredibly busy schedule, but I still make the time to teach karate to strippers for 3 hours a day, twice a day, every day.

This strip club is 30 miles from my 15-bedroom, 60-bathroom apartment. I could run there in 10 minutes. Or I could take my spaceship and get there in 5 seconds. But today I feel like driving my car.

I STEER THE CAR WITHOUT TOUCHING THE WHEEL. I USE MY TELEKINETIC POWERS TO NAVIGATE A SHARP TURN. THIS IS A GOOD WAY TO PRACTICE MIND CONTROL. THIS IS MIND OVER MACHINE.

I ALWAYS WEAR MY SEATBELT. NOT FOR MY SAFETY. FOR THE CAR'S. I'M NOT STRAPPING MYSELF TO THE CAR; THE CAR IS STRAPPING ITSELF TO ME.

THE BIRD SHIT ON MY CAR WINDOW GUARANTEES THAT NO ONE WILL MESS WITH MY CAR.

IF A BIRD SHITS ON MY CAR, IT'S GOOD LUCK. EVEN IF I INTENTIONALLY SCARED THE BIRD INTO SHITTING ON MY CAR.

I GO OVER THE AFTERNOON'S LESSON ON PAPER WITH THE GIRLS BEFORE WE PRACTICE. I'VE TAILORED THESE DRILLS SPECIFICALLY FOR THEM.

KARATE ISN'T ALL ABOUT FORM AND TECHNIQUE. THESE LADIES NEED TO LEARN THE REASONS WHY CERTAIN MOVES ARE BETTER THAN OTHERS. AND THEY NEED TO BE TAUGHT WHAT IT TAKES PSYCHOLOGICALLY TO BECOME A KARATE MASTER.

FOR THE FIRST EXERCISE, THE GIRLS KEEP THEIR TOPS ON.

Dancers face different dangers with their tops on than they do topless. The move I'm teaching here is the most effective way for a dancer to deal with a customer who has no patience for her to disrobe, and he erupts into violence while waiting for nudity to occur.

THIS MOVE ONLY WORKS IF THE LADIES ARE TOPLESS.

If you're a dancer reading this section, do not try to replicate this move with your top on. You could get hurt. This move is designed to punch out an oncoming attacker as you're kneeing a 2nd guy in the stomach while choking a 3rd guy whose neck is stuck between the triangular gap that your legs have made. It's one of the most difficult martial arts moves for a topless dancer to master, yet easy for anyone else.

THIS MOVE WORKS WHETHER THE DANCER IS TOPLESS OR NOT.

WE PRACTICE ELBOWING A CUSTOMER ATTACKING FROM BEHIND WHILE WE KICK A SECOND ATTACKER APPROACHING FROM THE FRONT.

I MAKE SURE EACH GIRL GETS THE PERSONAL ATTENTION AND COACHING THAT SHE NEEDS, NO MATTER HOW LONG IT TAKES.

CINDY IS WEARING HIGHER HEELS THAN SHE NORMALLY DOES, SO I SHOW HER HOW TO PROPERLY ADJUST THE ANGLE OF HER KICK. IT'S LITTLE DETAILS LIKE THIS THAT MAKE A BIG DIFFERENCE IN A FIGHT.

I FACE THE CLASS TO MAKE SURE THE GIRLS ARE USING PROPER TECHNIQUE.

"EXCELLENT FORM, HEATHER," I SAY.

SOMETIMES IT'S NECESSARY TO SINGLE OUT A STUDENT TO MAKE SURE SHE COMPLETELY UNDERSTANDS THE LESSON AND GETS IT RIGHT.

EVERYONE IS SUPPORTIVE AS LISA WORKS ON HER DOUBLE-KNUCKLE CHEST PUNCH. EVEN THOUGH THESE GIRLS SOMETIMES WORK INDIVIDUALLY, THEY MUST LEARN TO FIGHT AS A TEAM. THEY'VE ALL MASTERED THE POLE; NOW THEY MUST LEARN TO MASTER POTENTIAL ATTACKERS AS A GROUP.

I TEACH THE GIRLS HOW TO STOP AN ATTACK FROM THE OTHER SIDE OF THE STAGE.

THEY MUST HAVE THE AWARENESS AND SKILLS TO DEFEND ALL BORDERS OF THE STAGE.

The girls check their form in the mirror. Mirrors can be a helpful tool for working on proper form, but I don't recommend it. In most fight situations, you will not have the benefit of a mirror to help you. But there are mirrors at this club, so the girls must get used to working with them and learn to use them to their advantage.

I TELL A FART JOKE TO LIGHTEN THE MOOD.

THESE DRILLS ARE RIGOROUS AND CAN BE STRESSFUL, SO IT'S GOOD TO ADD SOME HUMOR WHEN TEACHING.

After the fart joke, I tell a personal anecdote. I tell them about a time when I was working security at a strip club and a gang of 20 bikers came in, and I beat them all up with one karate kick. But because of all the mirrors in the club, it looked like I beat up 200 bikers. Then I made them all blow each other and it looked like a 200-biker blowjob bonanza. My students get a nice laugh out of that story too. If you're teaching or doing charity work, telling a joke or funny anecdote can help the students bond with each other. <u>Learning how to defend yourself in horrifying, life-threatening situations can be a lot of fun.</u>

AFTER THE LESSON, I THINK ABOUT THE GRAVITAS OF TEACHING SELF-DEFENSE TO STRIPPERS.

I think about the hard work these women did, and how they came in 3 hours before their shifts started, just to study with me. Unlike the majority of people who do charity work, I don't do it because it makes me feel good or because it makes me look important, "hip," and "cool" to the general public. I do it because it's the right thing to do. I'm making a difference. Twice a day. This is a job I would do for free. And I do.

You must always remember what's important in life. There's more to life than just beating people up. There's also teaching people how to beat people up. I'm just trying to make the world a better place one karate kick at a time.

KARATE QUIZ

WHAT IS THE FIRST THING YOU NOTICE ABOUT THIS PHOTO?

YOU HAVE 1 SECOND TO ANSWER. WRITE YOUR ANSWER BELOW:

_____

_____

TURN TO THE NEXT PAGE FOR THE CORRECT ANSWER.

WITHIN THIS PHOTO, THE CORRECT ANSWER IS MORE EVIDENT.

If you wrote down for your answer "Judah Friedlander wearing his Campeon Del Mundo hat, waiting to attack me, while camouflaged in a messy room," you are correct. If you answered anything else, you are wrong. If this was not a book but a real situation, I could've killed you. I gave you 1 second to answer this question. Because that's how fast an attack can happen.

IF YOU DIDN'T SPOT ME AND LAUNCH YOUR ATTACK WITHIN 0.5 SECONDS, I WOULD HAVE DEMOLISHED YOU, AND YOU WOULDN'T EVEN KNOW WHAT HAPPENED.

Look at Photo 1 again. You didn't see me because I blended into the background and the foreground perfectly. Other instructors teach how to blend into the background, but I am the only person who teaches how to do both.

The purpose of this quiz is to teach you the importance of <u>analyzing a situation quickly</u>. Without quick analysis, all the technique I've taught you is worthless.

You've learned so much karate knowledge, you might be feeling overwhelmed and stressed out. Never get stressed. I've never been stressed. To be a master of the martial arts you must always be relaxed.

CHAPTER TWENTY:
CORRECT COOLDOWN
TECHNIQUE

THERE'S NO BETTER WAY TO COOL DOWN THAN WITH HOT CHICKS.

She's not diving. She's giving me an underwater massage with her mouth.

THIS IS NOT A HOT TUB. IT'S A REGULAR POOL IN MY SPACESHIP.

If you don't have a spaceship, then use a pool in another location. I set the water temperature to freezing. This is the cooldown phase, which means the water should be cool, not warm. The ladies and I heat up the pool with our sexual energy. When the water starts to boil, that's when I know the cooldown phase is over. I don't expect you to be able to do all of this, but try to start with the water cool and heat it up with a love partner.

I just had a 3-way with the girls who are passed out poolside. They're dreaming that one day they'll stir up enough energy to have sex with me again. After I make love to the rest of the girls, I'll lay their unconscious overheated bodies poolside so they don't drown. It's normal for girls to pass out after they have sex with me. They usually go into an immediate intense state of extreme ecstasy and then deep depression when they realize they'll never meet a man as sexually satisfying as me. In this photo, you can't see it, but I'm having a sexual experience with the one girl whose head is underwater. I wrote on the photo what she is doing.

I ASSIGN 2 GIRLS TO FOOT PATROL TO GUARANTEE THAT NO SOAP GETS ON MY RIGHT FOOT.

IT IS MY MAIN FIGHTING FOOT AND I DON'T WANT SOAP REMOVING ANY OF ITS ESSENCE.

Nicole and Nikki are my official Foot Patrol Team. Their job is to make sure soap never touches my foot. Being a Foot Patrol woman for The World Champion is an honorable position and is the highest paying job in the world of karate. I travel with these girls everywhere I go. Nicole makes 8 million dollars a week and her assistant Nikki makes 2 million a week just for guarding my foot during the cooldown phase. It's that important of a process. If you can't afford to hire 2 foot patrol girls, settle for just 1. And if you can't afford 1, then you must take extreme caution not to get any soap on your main fighting foot. The cooldown phase is about relaxing. When I have two gorgeous women guarding my foot from soap, it helps me relax.

Here's a photo from earlier when we all first got in the pool.

WOMEN WORSHIP MY WORLD CHAMPION BODY.

AND CRAVE MY KARATE FOOT.

When you have a body as orgasmically desirable as I do, and a foot that's killed a low estimate of 30,000 people, women sometimes don't know which to go for first. Only Nicole, the head of Foot Patrol, guards my foot, while her assistant Nikki gets a little more intimate with me. Pay close attention to how relaxed my face is. It's important to cool down your face muscles and not just your body muscles.

When the cooldown phase is over, I will hook up with more chicks so that I can warm up for bed time, where I will hook up with even more chicks. You should try and do the same thing.

A proper cooldown rejuvenates your body and gets you settled into a peaceful state of mind so that you're ready to beat up more people.

CHAPTER TWENTY-ONE: AFTER THE COOLDOWN: A TIME TO REFLECT

Another benefit of the cooldown phase, besides all the hot sex with beautiful women, is that it gives you time to reflect. Reflection is beneficial because it allows you to learn from your previous endeavors. Sometimes you need to look backward to move ahead. I thought about some of the fighting I've done recently. Especially about beating up the guy with 3 arms.

I decided to make a phone call to my new one-armed friend Joe. I told him that a few days ago I beat up a guy with 3 arms. Joe joked that I should have ripped the guy's third arm off and given it to Joe as a present. I said, "We should do that." Joe joined me and we went looking for the guy with 3 arms.

We went back to the exact spot where I beat up the 3-armed guy a few days earlier. Fortunately, he was still lying on the ground where I left him, and was just starting to regain consciousness. When he came to, he apologized for attacking me. I forgave him. He told me his name was "Teddy" but to call him "Fred." Fred and Joe bonded instantly because of their unique arm situation. Joe has no recollection of why years ago he woke up with a missing arm and Fred doesn't know why his body mysteriously grew a third arm one day. They're both unique individuals who unfortunately have been teased by other people just because they're different. I apologized to Fred for the overwhelming beating I gave him. And me and Joe forgot about previously wanting to detach Fred's 3rd arm so Joe could have it. I told Fred that he was cool and I'd give him free karate lessons if he pays for them up front. He agreed. We all hung out that afternoon and had a great time practicing fighting as a 3-man team. We're a good crew. Joe has 1 fist, I have 2 not counting my back-up fist, and Fred has 3. We're a team that's tough to strategize against. And we're all good buddies now. Joe and Fred are doubles partners in racquetball, and the 3 of us made a pact to team up every 6 months and pulverize criminals late at night. It's beautiful that <u>beating the shit out of people can create lasting friendships.</u>

We may never know why Joe is missing an arm, or why Fred has 3 arms, or why no matter how hard people try, no one will ever be as great a martial artist, an athlete, or as sexually desired and powerful as me. But we do know . . . that we're friends. And none of this would've happened if I didn't cool down properly and make time for reflection.

I put a photo of me, Joe & Fred in this nice frame.

Tough 'N' Tight

I'm saving the empty spaces for photos of our future adventures.

As you were looking at the above photo, I just did some more reflecting. And I realized something. I have more to teach you. So keep reading.

THIS IS MY KARATE ACADEMY.

You have to break through the brick wall to get in. And if you do, I'll be waiting inside to beat you up. That will be your first lesson. This is the toughest karate academy in the world. I've never had a student. It's always open. Enter if you can. Survive if you dare.

If you visit the psychic next door, she'll warn you to not even attempt entering my building. I agree with her. You should walk past my school and get a haircut at the barbershop instead.

THE MOST IMPORTANT PAGE IN KARATE HISTORY

ALL THE KARATE TECHNIQUE YOU'LL EVER NEED IS RIGHT HERE.

Throughout most of this book I don't go into the specific fundamentals of how to execute correct karate form. That's because I've done it all here. On this one page you will learn everything from how to make and use multiple fist formations to how to position each toe differently for each specific kick. There is more information on this one page than in any other karate book ever written. This page is 50 books within a book.

If the photos are too small and you're unable to read the notes I've written on them, then your vision is weak and you must improve it. If you need to use a magnifying glass, that's okay. It just means you're at a beginner level.

Memorize this page before moving on to the rest of the book.

THE MOST ACCURATE PUNCH IN THE WORLD

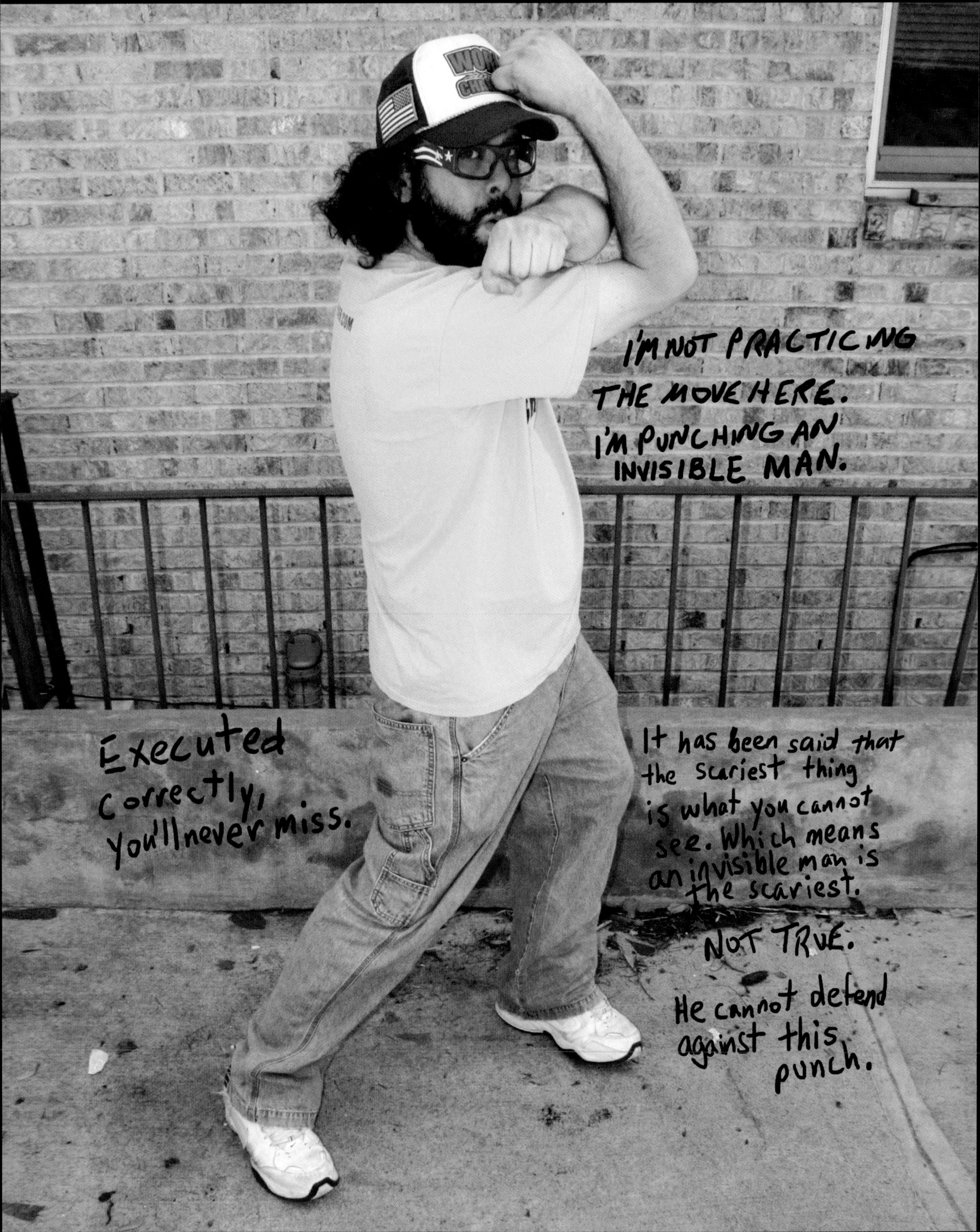

18 TRIANGLES OF POWER
18 is the most important number in karate.
Karate power eminates from the triangle.
21 is a winnnning number.
A triangle has 3 sides.
WORLD CHAMPION
WORLD CHAMPION
IF YOU FORM 18 triangles, you will always win.
Here's the proof:
18 + 3 = 21
21 → 2 + 1 = 3
18 → 8 − 1 = 7 and 7 × 3 = 21
18 → 1 + 8 = 9 and 9 ÷ 3 = 3
THAT is the secret of why 18 triangles gives you the winning power combination in Karate.
Karate has 6 letters. And 6 × 3 = 18.

SPECIAL CHAPTER: SHADOWS

My Karate skill is so perfect, you can learn a lot just from studying my shadow. You should probably study my shadow before studying me because it's slower than me. Which makes it easier to learn from.

I CAN CREATE A SHADOW AT NIGHT WHEN IT'S CLOUDY. DURING A BLACKOUT WITH NO LIGHTS.

I HIGH-FIVE MY SHADOW WHEN IT MAKES A GOOD MOVE.

DETACH

When least expected, I leave my shadow behind and do the fighting myself.

I CAN PUNCH A MAN'S SHADOW AND KNOCK HIM OUT.

KARATE PHILOSOPHY

IMPORTANT TIP TO REMEMBER

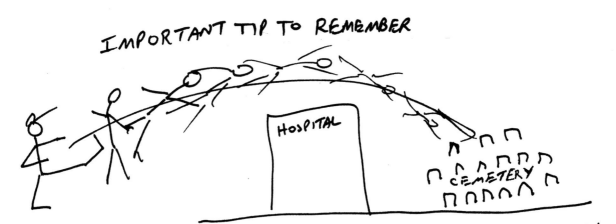

KICK YOUR OPPONENT DIRECTLY OVER THE HOSPITAL AND INTO THE CEMETERY.

ME BEATING UP A LIFEGUARD

HE DROWNS IN A TIDAL WAVE OF MY FISTS.

OTHER CHARITY WORK I DO THAT YOU CAN DO TOO.

I DONATE MY VICTIM'S BLOOD INSTEAD OF MY OWN.

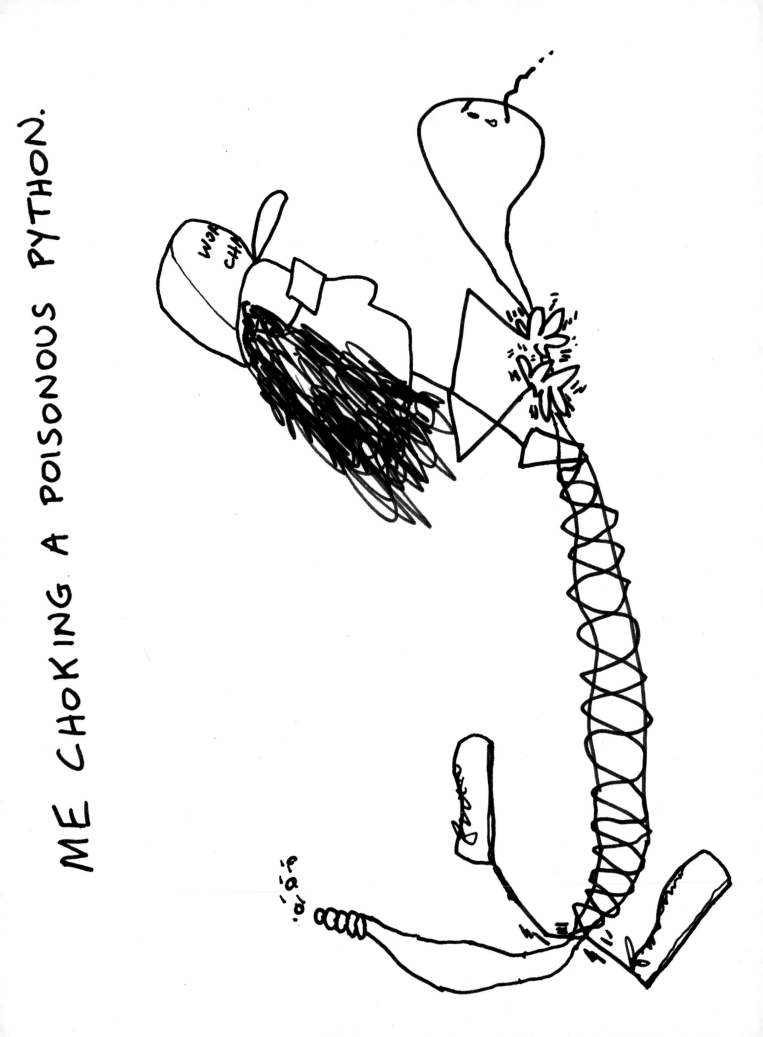

THIS IS WHY FLEXIBILITY IS IMPORTANT.

WHEN I KICK A DINOSAUR THIS HARD, HE CRIES BLOOD TEARS.

MY POWER KICK KEEPS THE DINOSAUR AT A DISTANCE. SOMETIMES I ONLY NEED TO SIZE ONE LEG. FOLLOW THROUGH ON YOUR KICKS SO THAT YOU KICK RIGHT THROUGH THE DINOSAUR.

It's almost the end of the book. I still haven't taught you everything I know. And that's the way I'm going to keep it.

Most books end with a boring wrap-up, restating all the stuff that was spelled out earlier. Well, this book isn't like most books. If you don't remember something, too bad. GO BACK AND LOOK AT IT AGAIN. And when you restudy a page, I guarantee you will find what you are looking for, plus discover something new that you didn't see initially.

It's time for you to stop studying and start using what you have learned.

YOU NOW KNOW HOW TO BEAT UP ANYBODY.

And on the next page is the certificate that proves it.

OFFICIAL CERTIFICATE
ROM THE WORLD CHAMPION JUDAH FRIEDLANDER

I KNOW HOW TO BEAT UP ANYBODY.

I, _____, have read The World Champion
Judah Friedlander's karate book and now know how to beat up anybody.
If I get into a fight and lose, it is not The World Champion Judah Friedlander's
fault. It is mine. I didn't study his book properly.

_____   _____
Sign Name   Date

WORLD CHAMPION APPROVED
NOT A PUSSY

Rip this page out and carry it around with you.
You can show it off to people and impress them.
If you use scissors to cut this page out, you're a
pussy, and this certificate is invalid.

CHAPTER INFINITY:
NOT THE EPILOGUE

What I'm about to show you in this chapter is not part of the lesson.

FIFTY THUGS AND A DIRTY COP DON'T SCARE ME.

IF YOU TRAIN REALLY HARD AND DEDICATE YOUR LIFE TO IT, YOU WILL ONE DAY NEVER BE ABLE DO THIS.

I KNOCK OUT 50 CRIMINALS WITH ONE KICK. REMEMBER: PUNCH TO PARALYZE BUT KICK TO KILL.

ANOTHER VICTORY FOR THE WORLD CHAMPION.

I COULD LAND, BUT I CHOOSE TO LEVITATE.

THE VIEW IS JUST TOO COOL FROM UP HERE.

Plus, I just got a call from The World Championship Committee and I have to be in Antarctica to defend my title in 30 minutes. Beating up these thugs turned out to be a good warm-up for my upcoming World Championship match. I'm going to win this one easily. I'm The World Champion and I can beat up anybody.

Keep training. You're a winner.

THE WORLD CHAMPION

BY JUDAHS CLONE FROM THE FUTURE

I know The World Champion Judah Friedlander because I am his clone and he just beat me up with one punch. My bloodied and disfigured clone-face is proof that a copy is never as good as the original. I'm only writing this backward because Judah said he'll beat me up even worse if I don't.

This is being written to you from the year 2153. 143 years after "How To Beat Up Anybody" was first published.

This is written backwards because in the future everyone is so self-centered that they only look at life through a mirror. They carry mirrors everywhere and never look at things directly. If you hold this page up to a mirror, You'll be able to read it properly.

It is the year 2153, manufacturing mirrors is the #1 money-making industry in the galaxy, besides "How To Beat Up Anybody". This book is still the best and most popular instructional karate book ever made. A First printing of this book is now worth over a trillion dollars. This book hasn't had any updates. It's never needed any. It is read to every unborn child when they are in their mothers' wombs. Everyone in the future has at least 3 copies of it. Often it is recited word for word from memory by couples in unison as they conceive a child. In 2085, "How To Beat Up Anybody" was officially printed on and along the entire length of The Great Wall in China in American English. As a result, American English is now China's #1 language.

Judah regularly travels here to the future in his time machine and gives Karate lessons to Robot Security Guards and Space Cops. Sometimes The Champ comes to the future without using a time machine — he just runs at bonus speed.

When Judah punched me 5 minutes ago, I thought, "That was exactly the way he explained it in the book". But I couldn't block the punch because he has studied this book more thoroughly than I have.

Plus, he's The World Champion and I am not.

I'm going to end this Backward now because Judah just told me to "Abruptly."

Sincerely,
But in a lot of pain,
The World Champions Clone
2153

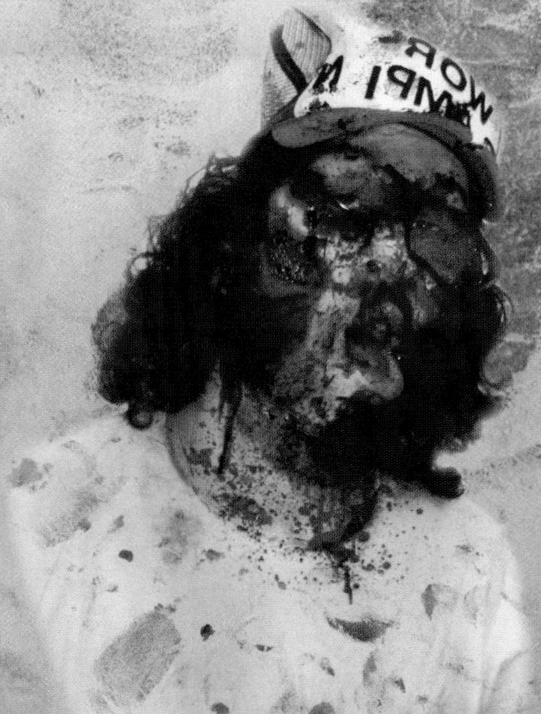

GLOSSARY

This book contains no glossary. Karate is about beating people up, not looking up words.

I forgot to mention that I wrote this entire book underwater in one sitting.

THE AUTHENTIC ACKNOWLEDGMENTS

Extra-special HUGE thanks to Shirley Friedlander, Arthur Friedlander, and Josh Friedlander. BIG thanks to Mike Weiss. BIG thanks to Kurt Iverson (digital effects and design work). I could not have made the book without all the help from the people mentioned above.

BIG thanks to everyone at It Books and HarperCollins. My editor, Kate Hamill; Carrie Kania (It Books publisher); Amy Vreeland (production editor); Lorie Pagnozzi (production designer); Sue Walsh (designer); Milan Bozic (jacket designer).

BIG thanks to everyone at Gersh Agency and 3 Arts Entertainment. My literary agent, Richard Abate; managers: Dave Becky, Josh Lieberman; agents: Bernie Spektor, Doug Edley, Jen Konawal.

All photography: directed by Judah Friedlander. All photographs are owned and appear courtesy of Judah Friedlander. All drawings and clay art by Judah Friedlander. Thanks to all the photographers: Angela O'Neal, Maja Leibovitz, Dexter Stallworth, Melissa St.Louis, Josh Petrino, Vanja Cernul, Bonnita Ann Bell, Howard Dover, Helin Jung, Josh Friedlander, Mike Weiss, Morgan C. Pitts, Alex Morgan, Russ Meneve, Paul Quinn, Lelani Lei Gibbs, Jon Gardner, Judah Friedlander.

Thanks to everyone who appears in the book. Jason Pollock (Bigfoot), Kazuyuki Yokoyama (ninja), Joe Adam (one-armed man), Rondell Hartley (3-armed man), Mad Dog Joe Stone (flipbook victim), Danny McDermott (male-pattern baldness punch victim), Marc Vivian (dislocated shoulder blade bully), couch ladies (Ninja chapter: Helin Jung, Brooke Lola Marie Maggie, Candice Fortin); Ravi Sagar Seepersad (man with sword and gun), Jared Rydelek (man with gun), Marvin Li (Karate Fart victim), Jack Krupey (stairway attacker), Dexter Stallworth (daytime mugger), Alex Morgan (night creep), Tahl Leibovitz (pizza delivery guy), Sean Pirzada (gang member), subway gang (from left to right): Grant Cooper, Vinny Cedeno Simon Kwok, Maja Leibovitz, Jordon Ferber (leader); Cooldown Chapter chicks: Laurence Gulyette Yang (Nicole), Lindsay Teed (Nikki), Heather Bunch (underwater mouth massager), MartiBelle Payano, Daveeka Sade, Fabiola Fung, Andrea Miele, Chelsea Marshall; Daniel Picciotto (unicyclist), rooftop victims (from left to right): Adeel Ahmed, P.J "Big Red" Landers, Steve Corcoran, Craig Loydgren; Cleve Manning (South American President), Michael G. Chin (Duke of China), James Hutchison (ball-kicked guy), Jason Mello and Jim Ng (guys lifted up by their balls); Jason Mello and James Hutchison (airborne muggers), James Ng (trash can victim), 50 muggers: Hector Genao, Adrian Goulet, Steven Jay Weisz (dirty cop), Ryan Dowling, Mark Dowling, Vincent Matheis, Luciano Janz, Ric Borja, Blaine Kneece, Alex Dziejma, Steven Sviridoff, Mik Thronveit, Dino Sossi, Michael Baez, Patrick Schramm, Cory Tervis, Sean Manning, Rolando Caraballo, Cory Jarvis, Mark Pagano, Peter Villahoz, Jamie Senicola, Joe DeLong, Isaac Betancourt-Sabillon. Eric Jensen, Sean Lavelle, Richard Mercuri, Vincent Shakir, Francisco Toribio, Sean Whiteley, Matt Pavich, Lance Svendsen, Reggie Wade, Santo D'Asaro, Rob Gordon, Frank J. Riley, Jesse Rafe Myerson, Mo Mozuch, Joe Pascuzzo, Ray Wagner, Zach Levin, Salvatore Cossart, Andrew Hillmedo, Joe Urban, Tim O'Neill, Andrew Hillmedo, Rob Gordon.

For Chapter Nineteen: Charity Work—special thanks to Susie Quigley and everyone at The Harem in Lodi, New Jersey. And the dancers from left to right: Heather, Savannah, Adrian, Cali Mack, Amber.

And more thanks to: Dexter Stallworth, Maja Leibovitz, Tahl Leibovitz, Yvonne Mojica, Laura Heywood, Josh Petrino (Bigfoot costume/makeup and additional digital gore effects), Yi Lin Ye (Mandarin translation), Judy Hugh, Lisa Qiu, Cecilia Leibovitz, Andrew Signoriello, James Lenzi, Brooke Lola Marie Maggie (beauty makeup for couch ladies and Cooldown chicks), Dan Paczkowski, Chris Ann Pappas, Paul Soule, Vincent Mallardi at Alcone Company, J. Travis and NY Health & Racquet Club, JR Ravitz, Tommy Zito, Annie Kuty, John Petrino, Cheryl Petrino, Jessie Swain, Peter Sabotka, Barbra Sabotka, Jason Katz, Mark Manne, Aaron Haber, Barbara McNamara, Aaron Seals, Arthur Dutkanicz, Abbie Hunt, Robert Michael Bell, Kevin Ladson, Eric Metzger, Morgan C. Pitts, Albert Cadabra.

If there's anyone I left out—it's accidental and I'll make it up to you with a free karate lesson.

HarperCollins books may be purchased for educational, business, or sales promotional use. For information, please write: Special Markets Department, HarperCollins Publishers, 10 East 53rd Street, New York, NY 10022.

FIRST EDITION

Library of Congress Cataloging-in-Publication data is available upon request.

ISBN 978-0-06-196977-5

10   11   12   13   14   DIX/QG   10   9   8   7   6   5   4   3   2   1

SPECIAL REMINDER: DON'T LITTER.

THROW TRASH IN THE TRASH CAN.

This page is left blank for your karate notes and questions that you'd like to ask The World Champion.

This page is not blank. The World Champion has written a secret karate message on it.

This page is not blank. It is filled with the screams of pain from everybody The World Champion beat up while making this book.

This page is not blank. It is filled with the thunderous mighty roar from around the globe for the triumph of justice that The World Champion's karate actions have served.

ABOUT THE AUTHOR

If you'd like to learn more about the author, read this book.